*The Devil's Looking-Glass*

'So it is a mirror, in the picture?'

'Course it's a bloody mirror. It's in the – '

'No, don't tell me. I'd rather not know. I was hoping . . . it didn't exist.'

'So first you saw your face in it, and then . . .'

'After I'd looked at my face for a while, the mirror got clearer, and then it turned away at an angle, as if something had jerked it round, and I got this astonishing sight for an absolute fraction of a second of a face staring up at me from the side. Someone much shorter than me, with a great shock of straight black hair and a . . . a wide face.'

'How wide?'

Born gestured with his hands. 'Too wide. Perhaps it was distorted, like the mirror, out of perspective.'

'Would you know it if you saw it again?'

'Would I bloody know it.'

*Simon Rees*

# *The Devil's Looking-Glass*

A Methuen Paperback

**A Methuen Paperback**

THE DEVIL'S LOOKING-GLASS

**British Library Cataloguing in Publication Data**
Rees, Simon, *1958* –
The devil's looking-glass.
I. Title
823'.914[F]  PR6068.E38/

ISBN 0-413-41440-X

First published in Great Britain 1985
by Methuen London Ltd
This edition published 1986
by Methuen London Ltd
11 New Fetter Lane, London EC4P 4EE


Printed in Great Britain
by Hunt Barnard Printing Ltd, Aylesbury, Bucks.

The Quotation from
*Journal of the Society for*
*Psychical Research* is reproduced
by kind permission of
The Society for Psychical Research.

The words to the song on page 79
are by Peter Davidson and are reproduced
her with his kind permission.

# *Romance*

*Defined according to*
*the Oxford English Dictionary*:

**3.** A fictitious narrative in prose in which the scene and incidents are very remote from those of ordinary life . . . in which the story is often overlaid with long disquisitions and digressions.

**5.** That class of literature which consists of romances: romantic fiction.

**6.** An extravagant fiction, invention or story; a wild or wanton exaggeration; a picturesque falsehood.

*Prior to each session, the subject filled out a pre-session questionnaire which enquired about initial relaxation, expectancy, mood, and motivation for success.*

*The subject then reclined on a mattress and was set up in an audiovisual Ganzfeld. Red light was diffused through halved ping-pong balls sellotaped over the eyes, and packed round with cotton wool, to create the visual Ganzfeld. The auditory Ganzfeld was created by relaying the output of a white noise generator through an Armstrong 521 amplifier using slope and bass filters into headphones worn by the subject. The subject chose his own level of sound intensity.*

Hugh T. Ashton, Peter R. Dear, Trevor A. Harley and Carl L. Sargent,
A Four-Subject study of PSI in the Ganzfeld,
*Journal of the Society for Psychical Research*,
Vol. 51 (1981–1982), 12–21 (p 13).

*This winter I was again employed by Lord Frederic Campbell, for I am an absolute auctioneer, to do him the same service about his father's collection. Among other odd things he produced a round piece of shining black marble in a leathern case, as big as the crown of a hat, and asked me what that could possibly be? I screamed out, 'Oh, Lord! I am the only man in England that can tell you: it is Dr Dee's black stone!'*

*Horace Walpole, Letters*, edited by W. S. Lewis,
48 vols (1937–83) XXIII, 286.

*But another important link connects Tezcatlipoca with obsidian. Bernal Diaz states that they called this 'Tezcat'. From it mirrors were manufactured as divinatory media by the wizard. Sahagun says that it was known as* aitztli *(water obsidian), probably because of the high polish of which it was capable . . . The name of the god means 'Smoking Mirror', and Acosta says that the Mexicans called Tezcatlipoca's mirror* irlacheaya *(an obvious error for* tlachialoni*) 'his glass to look in', otherwise the mirror or scrying-stone in which he was able to witness the doings of mankind.*

Lewis Spence, *The Gods of Mexico*, (1923) p 112.

# Chapter 1

After the final act, Wiston asked Gwyn Thomas why he thought Born had been so willing to go along with Thomas's plans. Thomas thought for the distance of three columns around the cloisters. Wiston, tall and angular in shabby grey flannels and tweeds, followed him half a pace behind, and waited patiently for an answer. He watched with distaste as Thomas's ears reddened under the strands of greasy hair, and caught himself looking for tide-marks round the neck, wondering when Thomas had last had a change of shirt. Wiston stopped his imagination turning to the state of his underclothes as Thomas replied.

'You see, it was his idea to participate . . .'

'In the séances?'

'I'd rather call them sessions. Sittings. They were to be very informal.'

'Not under laboratory conditions?'

'Not as such. And as for his work, he'd given all that up months ago.'

Thomas propped his shoulder against the pier at the

corner of the court, the nylon threads of his anorak catching on the rough stone. It was a sultry day, and the heat was rising off the river. Through the iron grilles in the library wall, Wiston could see the grey, oily surface of the water. The flagstones of the cloister were drying now after the morning's thunderstorm, that had felt like the last of all, an apocalypse.

'Was he jealous of you?' Wiston asked.

'Jealous? In what way do you mean?'

'You were up for a tenured post in the natural sciences. All he had was a temporary fellowship, in philosophy, running out this summer. He was a year older than you –'

'Two years older. Took a year off after school. Got out of phase.'

'You had a woman –'

'A wife, if you don't mind.'

'And he didn't, so that was another reason.'

'That's up to him, isn't it?'

*Careful with your tenses,* thought Wiston. *Past, present, future. Past imperfect, past perfect, past remote. But Born's in the present perfect, he has (just) died – and is still dead.*

'What about your seminar paper?' he pursued. 'Your famous article? Are you still going to let them print it? You'll have to be quick about stopping it, that journal's fairly prompt . . .'

'I've written to them.'

Wiston knew this: he had intercepted the letter on its way to the porters' lodge, and torn it up. Thomas's article would appear in the next issue of the journal, and that would be the end of him. Enough of amateurs dabbling in other people's fields. Amateur parapsychologists most of all. Let him get himself a job in industry, in a new town development area, with his wife and kids, where he could watch the telly and talk about molecules from morning till night.

'Did Born leave any papers?'

'Not apart from the ones you found in his room,' Thomas answered. 'And you've been through those, I believe.'

'As his executor . . .'

'Oh, yes, you're his executor, aren't you.' Thomas seemed angry. He scraped his shoulder round the stone pillar and walked along the colonnade, away from Wiston.

Wiston followed him, and laid a hand on his arm. Feeling the tension in the muscles, he could not decide if the facts had all sunk in, even with Born lying dead, even with the rumours that were on their way around the college like air-locks in the central heating, knocking on the pipes, filling each roomful of people with the news. They were alone in the court, but there was a head behind every curtain, a face at every window.

'Walls have ears.'

'And don't I know it.'

Thomas was calmer now, and let Wiston's hand stay resting on his upper arm. They walked together to the iron grille of the gate, and looked down towards the river. The first punts were feeling their way out after the rain, and a bright kayak, orange and blue, darted through the central arch of the bridge.

'Perhaps the less people know . . .'

There was an edge on Wiston's voice. Thomas turned at the next corner and shoved his handkerchief into his pocket. There was pollen in the air, even after the storm, and his eyes were streaming. He had had enough for one evening, but there would be plenty of time. They came through the archway into the river court, where the cars were parked.

'I'll say cheerio, then,' said Thomas, opening the door

of his white Ford Escort, streaked with the morning's mud.

'Till our next séance,' said Wiston, and smiled.

'Have your fun,' shouted Thomas. 'Have your bloody fun. If you want my advice you can go and get –' He slammed the car door, and tried to start the engine. It stalled repeatedly, the electric motor whirring and screaming in sharp bursts. Wiston walked away, rubbing his fingers on a smooth round pebble he found in his jacket pocket.

When he turned through the gateway, he saw that Thomas was out of his car and had the bonnet up. Wiston walked on down the avenue, towards the Fellows' Garden, and tossed the pebble into the grass. Halfway up the long nave of the green cathedral between the trees, that would start losing their first leaves tomorrow, he found himself following the ghost of Born, a tall black figure, like a mirage of darkness in the strong light. There was a roar on the road behind him, and Wiston stepped sharply to the side as the white car bolted past, ornaments bobbing triumphantly in the rear window and suspension clattering over the humps in the road.

Then he was gone, and Wiston followed the ghost – an image in his own eye – across the main road where he walked without flinching straight through the shiny black side of a remover's van – one that would soon return for his own belongings – and towards the wrought-iron gate into the garden. He paused at the gate and Wiston opened it for him, letting the slim figure slip past him and on up the path to the round pond, now covered almost completely by a thick growth of waterlilies: no flowers, only the padded green of the unreflecting leaves.

The moon was rising, and Wiston waited.

The ghost of Born, ignoring him, stood at the edge of

the pond facing the moon, and when Wiston went up behind him and touched his shoulder, he did not turn round. He was watching, in the ghost of the water, the ghost of the moon. Wiston felt himself watched in his turn, and looking up, saw that the moon herself had fully risen, and was facing him in the sky. He performed his usual obeisance, turned, and went back into college, where the bell was ringing for dinner.

Born's ghost was black, jet black, and almost invisible.

# Chapter 2

Born, John Born, lies on his back in his own set of rooms in the river court. They are large, spacious rooms, the windows on one side looking into lime-trees, and on the other almost obscured by a vast horse-chestnut whose pink candles have faded months ago and on whose branches bright green conkers with soft spines are forming, the nuts still creamy-white in their shells.

These are Born's last weeks in these rooms: he has occupied them for the past few years, on his research fellowship, years during which he has raised a mountain of logic from a molehill, and whittled it to a molehill again. Now he has little work and few friends: nothing left but time on his hands.

His face, Born's face, is a grotesque mask, something from the Greek tragedy or the modern revolutionary comic stage, a diagram of exophthalmia, a textbook illustration from a work on diseases of the eye, or a woodcut from a treatise on witchcraft. There is something shocking about his naked white eyeballs, as if they had been turned bodily round in his head like marbles, hiding the iris and the pupil.

Under their plastic covers, with jagged edges where Thomas cut round a ping-pong ball with a razor-blade to make two shallow cups, his eyes are dark enough, in the darkened room, to seem all pupil. The cups are tethered to his face by filaments of gauze, wisps of feathery tissue holding them down, like inflated tents at a fairground.

Over his ears sit the two squat shapes of the headphones, joined by a shiny black cable to the smooth, square-sided boxes of brushed aluminium in the corner of the room, now emitting, and to his ears only, the slow hiss of unmodulated vibration, the white noise from the generator that induces slumber, drowsiness, hallucination.

Born lies on the couch, his arms comfortably supported on cushions, a light coverlet keeping off draughts and regulating variations in temperature. His hands are outstretched, each in a padded cloth bag tied loosely at the wrist: he is supine, blind, deaf, quite helpless. He is not asleep.

Born is in the Ganzfeld, a state of semi-consciousness induced by lowering sensory input to a trickle: dim sound, dim light strain through the filters masking the ears and eyes, while keeping out the footsteps and voices in the court, the rustlings in the room, the bright flashes of sunlight that come intermittently through the leaves outside the window.

Under these conditions, crocodiles go drowsy, monkeys become excitable, and human beings, while not plunging into the screaming panic and unutterable horror of total sensory deprivation, show some signs of hallucination and bewilderment, and their sense of time and space goes slightly awry: something akin to mild schizophrenia, perhaps, or a light dose of LSD.

Much as Thomas would like to suspend Born in the

tank of luke-warm salt water in the upstairs lab at the Department of Human Physiology, in total darkness and the silence of the womb, until his sanity fails him, he cannot get his consent, and makes do instead with the makeshift equipment he can rig up in an ordinary college room, choosing Born's quiet set in preference to his own cramped, noisy quarters over the boiler-house. Besides, Thomas likes Born's room: it has a pleasant view and civilized furniture, a good desk with a green-shaded lamp, a Piranesi print in a thin black frame over the gas-fire, other prints of the colleges in passe-partout, the couch that would do to put up a casual guest, a dining-table with six chairs, and cases of brightly-bound books.

So Thomas sits at Born's desk, scribbling into a journalists' notepad with a chewed black pencil – one of Born's, out of a jar on the table in which, instead of flowers, grows an assortment of felt-tips, two draughtsman's pens, an ebony ruler and a stained clay pipe with scarlet wax on the stem – and watches Born. The slightest sign of movement, a twitch, a flexing of the muscles, the least yawn or sign of dropping off to sleep, and he will note it down. At last he bites at the end of his pencil, lets his breath escape with a hiss and draws a line across the bottom of the page.

'Well, we can call it a day now, I think.'

He snaps the notebook shut, pulls a thick rubber band down his wrist, over the back of his hand and around the cover, holding it firmly shut.

Born sat up on the couch, and pulled first one, then the other of the plastic hemispheres away from his eyes, loosening the sticky surgical tape from his eyebrows and wincing as it tugged the hairs away. He lifted the headphones carefully off and laid them on the couch, shaking his head like a man who wakes up in a railway compartment to find the other passengers staring at him. He pulled the bags off his hands, and looked around the room as if wondering whether he had missed his station.

'How long was I under this time?'

Thomas pulled back his sleeve over a hairy wrist, and pressed a tiny button at the side of his watch. The watch bleeped like a Mediterranean night-beetle, a faint white glow suffused the display panel and black figures showed against the light. 17:35:40.

'One hour, thirty-five minutes and forty seconds, to be precise, starting from sixteen hundred hours. That's the longest now by – let's see now . . .' and he opened the notebook again, snapping the rubber band, '– fifteen minutes and thirty seconds.'

'Were you bored?' asked Born.

He pushed his hand through his hair, which fell long and black between his fingers. His tie was loose around his neck: he did up the top button on his shirt and pulled the knot tighter.

Gwyn Thomas liked the way he dressed, his sportsman's easy way of filling out his clothes, the way his hair lay across his forehead – Thomas had a widow's peak and a thin patch over the crown – and the way he sat in a chair or walked across a room. He had seen Born naked once, swimming in the river, one day when he was taking his wife and children for a walk along the towpath: Born had waved at them from the water as if he had no shame in his nakedness, and Thomas, embarrassed before his wife, had not waved back. They met for the first time after that, in the college bar, and Born had teased him about it.

'Were you bored?'

'Bored?'

'Watching me. Can't be much excitement in that, can there?'

Thomas rubbed the bridge of his nose and stared at

Born, his forehead wrinkling.

'I wasn't watching you, John, I wasn't watching you at all. I was observing a phenomenon. You were simply the vehicle for that phenomenon, simply the medium. The phenomenon, the experiment if you like, was very interesting. Very interesting indeed.'

Born lowered his long legs over the side of the couch, and placed each foot carefully on the floor, as if he thought they might sink into the floorboards. *Foot's gone to sleep*, thought Thomas. *I'll make a note of that.*

Born shook his head again.

'It's so . . . disorientating. It sets your compass needle spinning, somehow, and when you get up, there's a moment when you don't want to . . . to take the blinkers off again, let the light in.'

Thomas squinted at him, his head slightly on one side.

'Better than the first time, then,' he said.

'Better. Odder, if that's what you mean. I can see the point in all this –' Born waved at the apparatus lying on the couch – 'if it can be guaranteed to bring on the kind of state you're talking about.'

'Better than a needle in the arm.'

'But it still depends too much on my own state of mind to be in any way . . . objective.'

'As I said,' said Thomas, 'I'm only interested in the mechanism. 'State of mind' is a subjective idea in itself. It isn't something I can measure electronically.'

'That's all that counts – electronic measurements? No questionnaires, no psychoanalysis?'

'Once I get you fitted up with a few electrodes, pressure detectors, thermometric sensors, that sort of thing –'

'You'll have me taped, eh?'

'I'll have you taped.' They grinned, and Thomas got up from the desk.

'If you're bringing in more equipment, won't that mean going to the physiology lab? And it isn't your department anyway, is it?'

'No, no, that's no problem, it's all portable. It isn't as if I was going to do a complete ECG on you.' Born raised one eyebrow. Light thunder rolled in the sky.

'Electroencephalogram. Measure your brain-waves. No, the first thing to do is to get you relaxed and receptive.'

'Sounds as if I need a massage,' said Born, and grinned again.

'You were much better this time. Hardly a twitch. I think we've got those padding problems sorted out. How were the eyepieces? Quite comfortable?'

'Quite comfortable, thank you, doctor.'

'No light seeping through the chinks?'

'No chinks to seep through.' Another grin. Born levered himself to his feet. The shape of his jawbone and the way his hair fell about his face gave him an expression, thought Thomas, that was slightly out of its time, seventeenth-century perhaps, or earlier. It reminded him of one of the portraits in the college hall.

'Tea, and music,' said Born, and he went, limping from the numbness in his legs, to fill the kettle at the tap in the kitchen. The door swung shut behind him, and a black shape remained in it, catching Thomas's eye: he turned and saw the random form of Born's gown hanging on a peg against the white paintwork, the ribbons and the two long sleeves with their cuneiform ends making an odd hieroglyphic that disturbed him.

A whining noise still came from the headphones, and Thomas got up to pull the jack-plug out of its socket in the amplifier and to disconnect the white-noise generator. He plugged in the speakers and switched the turntable on. There was a heavy double thud from the corners of the room, the stereophonic effect extending beyond the four walls, as if thunder had struck around and below them without a flash.

Thomas squatted on the floor to inspect Born's collection of records. The shelves above them were filled with slender, colourful volumes from the paperback shop, rows of green- and orange-backed thrillers, pointing up to the dull spines of books from the academic presses. He felt like a man without a garden who wanders into a seed-merchant's shop.

He turned to the row of records. How could a man survive without Bruckner, he thought, without Mahler and Brahms and the Bach organ works? All there was here was colourless, thin, austere music, to his taste: English folk-songs and the diagrammatic noises of the Second Viennese School. He found a compromise, shucked off the gaudy sleeve and balanced it on the turntable.

The music started. He went over to the window and looked out over the court. The only other lighted window, apart from the fortified slot of the porters' lodge, was Wiston's double casement beside the chapel tower, and Wiston himself was standing in the light with, Thomas thought, another figure behind him. As Thomas watched, Wiston reached up his arms and drew both curtains at once, shutting in the light. Thomas felt he had been caught spying, and turned back towards the shelves and the record-player.

Born backed into the room with a trayful of pots and cups.

'That was a present,' he said. 'You don't think I'd have actually gone out and bought an Elgar record, do you?' It was the 'Serenade for Strings'. 'Actually, that's a lie, I bought it for my mother, and then I remembered she doesn't have a gramophone.' He set the pot and the cups down on the polished top of the table and went out for milk and sugar. Thomas heard the slamming of the rubber-lipped refrigerator door, and poured out the tea.

'The milk's stolen, but nobody minds,' said Born, coming back with a half-empty bottle.

'I'll drink mine black.' Thomas squatted on the floor, and sipped his tea.

'Look what I found on the staircase,' said Born. He held out a long pale envelope with his own name carefully written in an italic hand. Thomas snorted.

'Isn't that Wiston's writing?'

'Wants me to dine with him tomorrow evening. In his rooms.'

'What's wrong with high table, that's what I'd like to know.'

'He just likes cooking for people, I suppose. I don't know, I've never been asked before. We're on chatting terms in the combination room, but that's as far as it goes.'

'Backs to the wall, then, chaps.' Thomas shovelled sugar into his tea, and stirred it vigorously.

'Nonsense, he's just being hospitable. You don't know him, do you?'

'By reputation only, I'm afraid. You'll be competing with him, I suppose, when it comes to the election?'

'Only indirectly. Why, do you think he wants to nobble me before the race?'

'It wouldn't be unheard-of.'

'That's absurd. His fellowship's on a different title, it'll be renewed automatically.'

'He might just want you out of the way.'

'Why? Do you?'

The music came to an end. Thomas drained his tea, and got to his feet.

'We'll call it a day, then? Same time tomorrow?'

Born nodded.

'You're not going to mention this to him?'

'To Wiston? Only if it comes up in the conversation.'

'Still early days, remember.'

'I'll remember.'

'See you, then.'

Thomas left the room and went down the stone stairs into the court, where he turned to look up at the window of Born's study, a brief glance to make certain that Born was watching him go, then went through the court to where he had parked his car, the grubby white Escort with the dice in the rear window, black and white, on a scarlet ribbon.

Born watched him as he drove away.

# Chapter 3

Born came to dine with Wiston the next evening. He sent a note in his neat handwriting, and one of the porters delivered it an hour before he arrived. Wiston had time to get the rooms prepared, rearranging furniture and ornaments, and lock the study door. A mixing of salad-dressing, a last look cast over the table, in case the informality should seem too studied, and then the knock at the door: enter Born in a dark suit and sensible tie, as if dressed for the memorial service of a remote acquaintance – himself, perhaps? – expressing, thought Wiston, an anxiety to please, even when it was too late.

'How nice to see you. We'll be waiting on ourselves this evening, just the two of us, quite familiar.' Wiston poured two glasses of very cold manzanilla, and Born raised his glass towards the window.

Wiston followed his gesture, and saw, through the pale sherry, the moon in the sky over the northern gate, inverted in his glass. Born turned, looking sheepish, and grinned when he caught Wiston's eye.

'It's obviously going to be a good evening,' he said. 'I

was expecting a note from you, I'm not sure why, and that's why I kept the time free. Why such a sudden invitation?'

'It seems the right time of year for impromptu pleasures, with the term over and the students away. Nothing to do but reading and writing, eating and drinking. Or whatever you find to amuse yourself.' Born felt the words rise into his mouth, to tell Wiston what he had been doing, to let out Thomas's secret, but was stopped in time by Wiston's next remark.

'I'm such a fool. I'm doing the cooking myself this evening, but I've forgotten to tell them to bring up the wine. Do excuse me for just one moment while I pop down to the buttery. Sit yourself down and look over some of those pamphlets in the corner, if you like. And help yourself to sherry.' Wiston waved him over to a pile of old catalogues from auctions and exhibitions, and backed out of the room.

Born wrote to his mother later on that evening: Wiston read this letter, and many others, during Born's illness and after his death, with her permission.

'. . . How can I describe Wiston? I've told you that he's tall, early forties, the archetypal bachelor don. They've had them here for centuries, only in the old days they'd have taken holy orders, which must have suited them . . . wears his jackets to ribbons and patches them along the seams, the oldest flannels, shirt-collars worn through, the rags of a stripy tie , . . He looks immaculately dressed from about ten yards away, but if you come any closer you can see . . . but no one ever does come any closer, which seems to be half the trouble. Lonely, yes, but in an odd sort of way, as if being with other people drained him out: he only seems to tolerate company at the table, as if he needed nourishment to keep him from going under . . . Thin face, colourless hair, looks sixteen or sixty depending on the light, one of those faces you could draw in three strokes with a stick in the sand – nose, chin and cowlick of hair. Coat-hanger shoulderblades, and the longest, thinnest, driest hands you ever saw, with a waxy look about the knuckles, and nails bitten right to the quick.

'He set me to look through a mountain of catalogues, twopence-coloured from Christies and Sothebys, penny-plain from the local auction-rooms, mostly furniture, mirrors, drab English portraits, that sort of thing. I particularly noticed the mirrors, as he had marked them in the margin and noted the prices and what looked like the names of the purchasers, and dog-eared the tops of the pages. The oddest thing about it was that whenever there was a picture of one, he had scribbled a face in it – not a nice face, I would have said, and certainly not his own – but I suppose he'd been doodling idly to fill up a lull in the bidding.

'Looking around the room, I could see where that sort of taste leads to: he has some good pieces, mostly heavy English stuff, a nice bow-fronted cabinet, a set of Queen Anne dining-chairs and table, some dark gloomy portraits in plain wooden frames, ecclesiastical dignitaries out of the college store. But the furniture was his own: the only other stuff of that quality here is kept in the Master's Lodge.

'The rest of the room was rather dull, so when I had finished my turpentine – *I'm sorry about the sherry*, Wiston noted, *I thought he'd like something on the dry side* – I tried the door of the study, but he had locked it, which seemed an odd thing to do. Nothing so tempting as a locked door. When I'd rattled it a bit I heard him coming up the stairs, and went and sat down with my catalogues like a good boy.

'It surprised me to see how tall he was when he came

into the room, quite a shock to catch him lowering from the doorway about six inches taller than I thought. Then I noticed the step down into the room. An odd effect all the same. He had a great dusty cardboard box full of bottles, not all for us as it turned out . . .'

Wiston set the box down on the sideboard. Born saw him glance about the room, and was glad the books were all in their places. Wiston peeled the lead foil from one of the bottles, folded it into a pellet which he pocketed carefully, and prepared to draw the cork.

'I do hope you weren't too dreadfully bored waiting. I find those old catalogues quite good fun in their way.'

'I can see you don't keep them just for the pictures.' Born laid a hand on the back of one of the dining chairs, and patted the wood.

'Oh, I occasionally splash out, as you can see, but you can't do much these days on an academic stipend. Though one can find ways of stretching it.'

The cork popped, and Wiston blew the dust from the neck of the bottle. He thought of another remark.

'Your mother lives alone, now? Not too far away?'

'Not too far, not too near. We keep in touch.'

Wiston laughed, and went to draw the curtains.

'It's a very simple supper this evening, I'm afraid; just an omelette, cold chicken, salad, rice pudding. Plain, purificatory food.' He went into the kitchen and lit a gas-ring; Born could hear it roaring as he put the match to the flame. Now that Wiston's back was turned, he went to the study door, and tried it again.

'That door is locked,' said Wiston from the kitchen, breaking eggs with one hand into a china basin. 'You'll have to wait till after we've eaten. Can you sing?'

'For my supper? Yes, if I have to. I'm rotten at sight-reading, though.' Born hesitated, then – 'I did try the door, it seemed irresistible.'

'Locked doors always are.' Wiston beat the eggs with a whisk. 'I keep my instruments in there.'

'Instruments?'

'Old keyboard instruments. Spinet, clavichord, fortepiano. What sort were you thinking of?'

Born did not answer the question, but asked another. 'Gosh, all on an academic stipend?' He felt it to be an indelicate remark.

'There's been the occasional windfall, the odd thing that turns up from time to time. One doesn't do too badly. But tell me, can you sing?'

'I've bellowed away in choruses.'

'You make it sound like a field sport.'

Wiston came in with the omelettes, and they sat down to eat. Born noticed that the knives and forks – silver and of an old design – were too dull to show a reflection: sulphur from the eggs, he supposed, and remembered sitting on the floor in his mother's house, as a small child, with a bottle of silver-dip, a soft cloth and a canteen of tarnished cutlery, polishing the handles and cleaning between the prongs. They ate in silence. There were chunks of white bread in a basket, but no butter, and the salad was of bitter leaves, red lettuce, endive and sorrel from the market, with good oil and lemon juice. They both drank well, and soon had to open another bottle. Wiston wiped his plate clean with a bit of bread, and went into the kitchen, returning with a cold roast fowl and a bone-handled carving-knife with dark blotches on the blade. He tested the edge on his thumb, and began to dismember the bird.

'You're coming up to the end of your stay here, I believe?'

'That depends on how the elections go.'

'I'm in the same position, under the new seven-year rule. O for the days of stipendiary life-fellowships, eh?'

Wiston worked the blade between the hip-joint and the carcase, and lifted the leg on to Born's plate. 'I suppose we'll be in competition, then, in a manner of speaking.'

It seemed to Born that they were hardly in competition: Born read philosophy, Wiston was an historian when he was anything at all, so there seemed little enough reason . . . *Damn the man,* he thought, *just like him to use his hospitality as a lever . . . but how else is it ever used?*

'I can't see there'll be much of a problem, can you? They're unlikely to give you the push after all this time.'

'Ah, these scientists can be a rule unto themselves,' said Wiston, waving the carving-knife playfully and darting his fork into the parson's nose. 'Unless you spend all day in a laboratory and talk about molecules, they can't see any justification for having you around the place. We might as well be at a polytechnic for all the co-operation we get. And they're in a majority, you know. Your friend Thomas, now . . .'

Born had a mouthful of food, and swallowed it before replying.

'He's the last person to stand in your way or mine. Quite sympathetic to the arts, I would have said. After all, his hobby . . .'

'Ah, yes, I've heard rumours. Parapsychology, isn't it? Things that go bump in the night. He's a Welshman, I understand. Ah, well, the Celtic temperament . . .'

They ate silently for a while. Born licked his front teeth, and pursed his lips.

'But it'll be a formality, naturally. Your reappointment, I mean.'

Wiston thought for a minute by the clock before replying.

'No, I think I shall be on my way, as friend Thomas would say. I've had my seven years. I shall pack my boxes, call the removers, and shift the circus off to its next location.' This statement surprised Wiston himself, as if he had come to the middle of the sentence and found the decision already made. Born had finished his chicken, so he cleared the plates away and clattered the bones into the kitchen rubbish-bin. He came back with a dish of rice-pudding with a brown crust of nutmeg on the top.

'But you must never given way to the Thomases. That was really why I asked you round to supper. I want you to spike their guns.'

Born laughed, and helped himself to the pudding, with a light crunch as the spoon broke through the crust. *I chose the food well,* thought Wiston. *A taste for nursery cooking is always a good sign, and Born has the true look of an epicure in the making: give him another ten years in the place, and all he'll want is his dinner . . .*

'Now, tell me, I'm dying to know, what have Thomas and you been up to these last few afternoons, burning daylight with the curtains drawn? It has caused some comment in the lodge, I don't mind telling you. It sounds as if you've been holding a séance.'

Born reddened.

'It's all to do with his latest piece of research. I think Thomas is just feeling around the subject at the moment, looking for a soft spot to penetrate.'

'And you're helping the operation?'

'I'm providing an open mind.'

'A *tabula rasa* for his stylus?'

'If you like.'

Wiston raised his eyebrows, and went to the kitchen for fresh glasses, a basket of fruit, cheese, biscuits and a decanter of port with a silver label. *Tarnished too,* thought Born, *like everything else.* The percolator hissed on the gas-ring; Wiston wrapped his hand in a dishcloth to protect himself from the steam, and poured coffee into two small heavy cups that looked stolen from an Italian espresso-bar.

'We'll drink our coffee in the music-room,' said Wiston, giving Born the tray to hold while he fiddled with the key, which hung from a heavy chain clipped to his fob-pocket. *Odd,* thought Born; *I wonder if he keeps his bedroom locked.*

He confided this thought to his mother, in the same letter, and continued:

'We went into the study, or music-room, and if the furniture in the dining-room was good, the stuff in there was better. I started looking around, but Wiston just waved his hands vaguely and said something about family heirlooms. There was a pair of heavy silver candlesticks on the ledge over the fire, pitch black and covered in wax and – now here's a queer thing – the wax was black too.

'He went across, lit the candles and turned off most of the lights in the room, then we sat down at the table and drank our port and our coffee. I kept looking around the room, as he didn't seem anxious to talk. The instruments were good enough, though I'm no connoisseur. No pictures to speak of, not that I noticed at first.

'The finest things in the room were the mirrors: a great cheval-glass over the fireplace, a huge, warped, smoky affair that I didn't like to catch my face in, and a smaller one between the windows. Two or three others had curtains over them, but I suppose he'd done that in the storm and forgot to draw them back – we've had a lot of thundery showers and scattered outbreaks of rain, as they say, over the last few days. Oh, and a little convex glass set into the panel, which could have been as old as the room: it looked as if it had a frame, but that was just the way the panel had been carved around it. It looked like the mirror in the Arnolfini painting – but without an inscription.

'We had got to our third glass of port, and what with all the wine I'd drunk with the meal and the general atmosphere, I was beginning to feel the effect. He watched me all the time. There was something about the room, as if he had been burning incense or some kind of drug – perhaps it was the candles. I had the feeling that if you rolled the carpet back . . .

'Fortunately we got off the subject of Gwyn Thomas and the afternoon sessions: I didn't like his tone on the matter, something nastily suggestive, indecent, almost. I feel he has a grudge against Thomas, against scientists generally. Then he went across and opened the lid of an old square piano – I made some quip about always being able to tell a Broadwood by the broad wood pedals, but he could see I'd read the name on the front – and began to tinkle away. I was thumbing through some of the sheet-music on the table, and asked him if he had any of the pieces you and I used to go through at home, "Is my Team Ploughing?", you know the kind of thing. No he hadn't, not to his taste at all, knuckles rapped all round. He found some Elizabethan airs in a big red-bound edition, and began a most melancholy piece while I warmed up by singing scales to "la" and that nice tricky "Cricket Critic" tongue-twister we used to do with the chorus. Then we went through half a dozen songs and some catches, but he would keep going back to just two pieces, "Take it again from the top", he'd say, no "shall we" about it: "Flow my Teares" was one – note the authentic spelling, there's scholarship for you – but the other was a mad lover's song that I never want to hear again as long as I live, let alone sing it, all eerie runs and trills and arpeggios up to the top of my register – and past it, too – and a final fading cadence that made me want to die away and follow it for good.'

Born had a pretty voice, chorus-trained and evidently used to singing with his mother beside the domestic piano, a fairly light tenor that floated the top notes but came through strongly in the middle register: it suited the songs very well, thought Wiston. How did the words go?

*'Hark you shadows that in darkness dwell:*
*Learn to condemn light,'*

sang Born, cracking the top note,

*'Happy, happy they that in Hell*
*Feel not the world's despite.'*

Not perhaps a cheerful song, but a good one, quite well suited to an after-dinner sing-song on a summer night. Wiston had left the windows open, behind the curtains, so the sound should have travelled well across the court, in the moonlight.

*'Know, know where shadows do for bodies stand*
*Thou mayst be abused if thy sight be dim.'*

Born's letter continued:

'It was at this moment that I noticed a couple of rather creepy pictures on the wall, between the end of the piano and the keyboard of the spinet. Don't ask me what was in them, as I couldn't work them out at all, but they seemed to be a pair, both views of some kind, through arches that went high up into the sky, with little dwarfish figures running about underneath. I had the feeling that each was the same view as the other, but seen from the wrong side of the arch. As if the arch were the frame of a mirror – but such a mirror! I don't like to think about them. In fact there was a mirror hanging between them, with a rather similar frame, so perhaps that was what put the idea into my head. It was tarnished, too, like everything else, and the odd thing was, although I was standing in front of it –'

Here the letter breaks off abruptly, with a note in Wiston's hand: *I have cut this passage, as Born becomes very foolish, showing the first signs of that weakness of mind that was to become so sadly apparent later on. If he had been trying to find an excuse for poor sight-reading, these remarks would have been understandable.*

In the end, Wiston let Born sing his Butterworth and Britten, which he kept hidden away in the piano-stool: he romped through them quite creditably, and seemed to cheer up at once.

'Jolly nice evening,' he said, at the end, after they had folded up the music again. His face was still ruddy, but for a different reason, as if he had just come back from a long run in the rain. *Quite a sympathetic look,* thought Wiston, *for a puppy.*

'You must come again,' he said sincerely, before Born could issue any invitations of his own. 'And you might like to take this away with you for some bedtime reading. I find that working through the Italian helps one get to sleep.'

It was another catalogue, this time of an exhibition, or series of exhibitions, held in Florence to celebrate the later Medici, for which they must have ransacked every Renaissance collection in Europe and America. This particular catalogue described the scientific achievements of the age, and was copiously illustrated with colour-plates and half-tones, with many scholarly notes and appendices. Wiston slipped the catalogue into a large manila envelope, and wrote his name across it, not knowing quite why he did this, but feeling that it was the thing to do, then sealed the flap.

'You might find this comes in useful, if you ever need a

picture-book. There are some nice things from various English collections, particularly the British Museum, well worth looking out for. And, by the way, while I think of it, there's an auction next Saturday, out in the country. You can drive me there. I'll see to all the arrangements. Now don't argue. It's well past your bedtime.' He shook Born's hand, and held it for a second too long.

'I'll certainly come,' promised Born, and thanked him many times. As he ran away down the stairs and across the court, Wiston sat at the keyboard of his Broadwood square piano and played, very softly, Tompkins's 'Sad Pavane for these Distracted Times'.

# Chapter 4

Thomas went to Born's rooms on the morning after the dinner, early enough to show that he was curious about what had happened the night before, but late enough to be certain that Born would be up and dressed.

Born did not want to answer any of his questions, so Thomas, feeling snubbed, went into the corner with the amplifiers and began to set up the silver boxes and trailing wires of the apparatus he had borrowed from the laboratory. He tried to stabilize the flickering green line on the black face of the oscilloscope by turning and tuning the horizontal and vertical shift controls, and fiddled with a red-handled screwdriver in the back of the machine. He fixed a cap-like device with trailing wires extending from beneath it to a long lead, which he plugged into another silver box, connecting the whole apparatus to a tape-recorder. Then he looked up and stared at Born.

Born, haggard and hung-over from the night before, was sitting at his desk, writing a letter to his mother. He wrote with a ball-point, and leaned on an old colour-supplement magazine, a Mexican issue with an Aztec figure on the cover. Thomas watched him satirically.

'Writing a letter to Mum, then, are you? All about how this mad Welshman's got you trapped in durance vile, after a night at the pub, making you have visions of diabolical blandishments?'

Thomas liked annoying Born by turning up the touch of Welshness in his voice, lingering over the consonants and lilting the vowels in certain words to punctuate a comment or to make a point. It irritated Born just as he intended.

'Come on, sign off now, send her love and kisses.'

Born clicked his ball-point briskly and folded the letter in three.

'Are you all set up and ready, then?'

'Yes, we're off for a trip round your cerebral hemispheres, if you've got any left after last night's carousings. So you can stick a stamp on your envelope, and we'll get right on with it.'

Born put the letter into the top drawer of his desk, went over to the couch and picked up the cap with the electrodes.

'I won't need my head shaved?'

'Just a dab of graphite on the temples, that's all, to improve the conductivity. Nothing you need to worry about.'

'I've heard that one before. If I knew more about the point of this experiment –'

'You'd mess it up completely. You don't need to understand, in fact it's better if you don't. You'll be more relaxed and more receptive. Otherwise you'd end up falsifying the evidence, you couldn't help it. This isn't like a lie-detector, if that's what you're thinking. More like one of those ink-blot tests. If I told you what to look for, you'd see it, whether there was anything there or not. Anyway, you've read that article I gave you. That tells you all you need to know.'

'Am I supposed to be being intelligent?'

'No, just observant, receptive. We're dealing with the threshold of consciousness. You're my most sensitive piece of measuring equipment. The rest of this stuff is junk in comparison. Like using opera-glasses for astronomy, or trying to take your temperature with an oven-thermometer.'

'So this is more in the realm of psychology than neurophysiology?'

Thomas folded his hands in a lecturing attitude.

'Psychology, parapsychology, they're just names. My interest is the brain, how it works, how cerebral functions leave chemical, electrical traces – though it's the electrical ones we're measuring here.'

'Brain-waves, you mean?'

'If you like. I'd hate to try and be more specific – it's really outside my field. There's no point in speculating when you've got so little data on how the brain actually works. You can tell more about it from its mistakes, that's what I'm driving at, so we're trying to give it something it isn't used to handling, mild sensory deprivation, the so-called Ganzfeld effect, meaning a pleasant background field of sensation, and see how it responds.'

'See how I respond, you mean.'

'I'd sooner say "it" in this context. You see, it's the mechanism that concerns us.'

'And what if I flip my lid?'

'That's so unlikely, it's almost impossible. You'll be quite well enough occupied, looking and listening out for odd variations in the normal thought-patterns, small irregularities in the field . . .' Thomas passed his hand across the couch, smoothing it out. *Feeling for 'irregularities in the field'*, Born thought, and smiled.

'There's far more chance of your accommodating yourself to this than to full sensory deprivation, that's for certain. I've seen some people who tried that.'

'Not a pretty sight?'

'Not pretty at all. This . . . well, it's more like trying to rationalize your dreams, to work out where the individual elements come from, and where they all fit in.'

'What if the dream's a nightmare?'

'You'll still find some pattern you can follow.'

'If I wake up screaming, though, you'll know what's gone wrong.'

'You won't be asleep, so how can you wake up?'

Born went to the couch and lay down, while Thomas busied himself around his skull, fixing the cap of wires, dabbing graphite-powder on his temples and taping down the electrodes, putting the covers over his eyes, adjusting the headphones and setting the white-noise generator to send a faint, stereophonic hiss into his ears.

Lying there, Born felt his head expanding, bellying out like a hot-air balloon with the burners going, floating him up. He signalled with his hand, and Thomas went with his notebook to the desk.

Born kept some notes of the proceedings himself, in a green-backed notebook which Wiston later found in another drawer of the desk.

'This is the first time I have felt it really working. Once the sensation of lying or standing or sitting has stopped, and I have lost the sense of direction, any idea of relative size stops as well. It does not seem to matter how tall or how heavy my body is, or what time of day it is, or whether it is winter or summer. I am circling around the one idea I know, the idea of myself, but the problem is that there is no idea, no self, just a circling motion, no consciousness of presence or absence.

'As far as I was aware of the passage of time during this session, this was the sequence of events. First, when the electrodes were fixed, there was a sensation of coldness at the temples, and a tingling as if an electrical current were passing. This is absurd, I know, but that is what I felt. My eyes grew hot under the plastic covers, the halved ping-pong balls, and the edges were sharp and dug into the orbital bones around the eyes. But the light was uniform and regular, a faint white light, no pink or yellow in it at all, and none of the black specks in the eyeball that disturbed my concentration last time.

'The sound in the headphones – again, it was hard to judge its intensity, as there was no particular tone to fix on, but after a while certain frequencies became more pronounced, a minor chord if anything. It reminded me of the harmonies in the songs we had been singing the night before, and I found myself straining to pick out anything more definite. It was like trying to tune in to a distant short-wave radio station, the same rising and fading of the signal, and the same background hiss.

'There was a feeling of being drawn upwards and outwards, and a pressure-change in the ears, as if the headphones had been suction caps, or as if we were flying at a high altitude and the plane had depressurized suddenly. I know now what it is to be deaf, hearing nothing but internal voices. My eyes felt drawn, too, and started to water.

'This was the peak of discomfort on this occasion, and the peak of sensation: after that, my concentration started to break up. One image, though, came through particularly strongly. I couldn't place it at the time. but afterwards I realized what it was: the Aztec figure on the cover of the magazine on the desk. Thomas must have been staring at it the whole time, which is odd. I mentioned it to him after I had called him over, while he was taking off the wires and dismantling the apparatus. He seemed quite pleased, and made a note about it. I had been under for an hour and fifty minutes, a good improvement.'

# Chapter 5

Country-house auction-sales attract the best and the worst elements in any area, Wiston explained to Born as they drove out of town in a borrowed car. The best come from the nearby villages, where people still expect to buy good solid usable furniture at bargain prices when a family is selling up, and the worst are the dealers from distant towns who come vulturing in whenever there is a whiff of carrion from relatives hurrying to beat the death-duties and sell off what they can. They come down in parties, but take care to arrive one by one, so they can form a ring and meet up privately after the sale to hold another auction of the goods, in a woodland clearing or among the sand-dunes, if the sale is at a seaside town. Second-hand books and furniture bring out the dissecting interest, Wiston propounded: so often are they worth more cut up and sold piecemeal, or falsified into something more valuable. Why had he brought Born along? Not to bring out the predator in him, nor to use his skills as a porter, or a chauffeur, but because he had shown an interest in the auction pamphlets, because he sang prettily, because Wiston liked . . . his company.

The car he had borrowed was long, black and shiny, almost a limousine, far wider and longer than the narrow streets of the town, let alone the country lanes, would comfortably accommodate. It belonged to one of the senior Fellows whose driving days were over, and it regularly stood by the main gate with a sticker on its windscreen warning the traffic-wardens that they might not have it towed away and impounded. It took Born some time to get used to the steering: the sheer length of the car made it clumsy in cornering, but it had a fair turn of speed on a straight stretch of road. Born liked the way it rode past the smaller traffic, the air-horn scattering cyclists and pedestrians and the six-cylinder engine roaring under the bonnet.

Wiston met Born at the gate with a picnic-hamper as the clock on the chapel was striking nine; the thundery weather had passed over and the cobbles were dry: it looked set to be a fine day.

'We'll load this into the boot,' he said, indicating the hamper with the toe of his shoe, 'and then we shan't need to worry about dashing away. These sales start early, and most of the interesting stuff will have gone by noon, so we shall have an hour to get there, an hour to look, an hour to bid, an hour to eat, and be back here again by two.'

'Quite a plan of campaign. And plenty of room in the car to carry home our spoils in triumph.'

'That rather depends on the determination of the London dealers, who are bound to turn up: if there's anything really good they'll have heard about it on the grape-vine, and you can forget about bargains. The moment a stranger starts bidding they'll just send the prices up to spite him. But we might be lucky. That's the point of the car: it's large enough to make them think we've come on business – which we have – and opulent enough to terrify the smaller operators, who will turn up in the firm's rusty hatchback and park it out of sight, into thinking that the bidding will skyrocket the moment I put up my hand. That should keep them off what I want. And the fact that I shan't be bidding for everything will make them imagine I'm a specialist, and that always helps the deception.'

'You seem to have your tactics well worked out.'

'Strategy, strategy, part of a lifetime's plan,' said Wiston with an agreeable pomposity, allowing himself to sink back into the leather upholstery as the car took to the road.

'So we're off for a serious day's buying?'

'You don't think I'd have wasted your time on a wild-goose chase? At the very least, I shall have to find something to reward your pains.'

'No pains, sir,' said Born, smiling at the face in the mirror, like someone who had been taken on excursions before, not just by avuncular dons, and had come off the better for it. *Innocence and corruptibility go well together*, thought Wiston, *and innocence is a thing I like, if it drives well*.

'There is a stretch of motorway I'd like you to avoid,' said Wiston, after they had been driving for half an hour. The countryside was changing slowly from flat fenny plains to chalk uplands. Wiston stared happily at the view out of his side-window, as if it were a pleasant moving picture projected on to a wall for his amusement. 'Country lanes and large cars can be quite fun, don't you think, when there's no risk of getting held up behind a combine harvester.'

Born nodded, and told an anecdote about a farming uncle, or great uncle, who drove his Daimler across his own ploughed fields, to try out the suspension. Wiston decided he would buy him a sporting print. The country flattened out, fell into folds, and flattened out again. Columns of smoke, like typhoons seen from a distance, rose out of the strawfields where stubble was burning, and propped up the heavy stormclouds that were gathering again, obscuring the sun.

'I have a feeling we'll be picnicking indoors,' said Born.

'Camping out on a bare floor in an empty room, with the chandeliers in sacking, and faded patches on the walls where the pictures have been.'

Wiston unfolded a map, which was merely a diversion, as he had worked out the route in advance. The side-roads were indeed the best ones to take, as they had seen no rival traffic – but just as Wiston was folding up his map again, and his view through the windscreen was blocked, a sports-car with the roof down overtook them, horn blaring, and forced the black limousine into the side of the road. It was a surprisingly deep horn for so small a car, thought Born, and smiled at his own surprise, then bit his lip: a small humiliation in a large car is always more infuriating, more unanswerable than a major outrage suffered in a Mini. To calm his feelings, he began to hum a tune. Wiston recognized the tune: it was the song by Dowland, 'Flow my Teares', and it lasted until they came to the gates of the house.

Later Born wrote to his mother: 'There was the little sports-car drawn up with all the others, and I can tell you, I was tempted to drive up alongside and scrape its panels. No sign of who was driving it, and I hadn't been able to catch a glimpse of him as he overtook us. I could see Wiston peering over the crowd to see if he could catch sight of him, too – at least, I assumed it must be a man. There was a fair turn-out, and Wiston was right about who would be there: all the locals dressed in their

Sunday best and poking about the grounds, while the dealers had dressed up for a day in the country in their tweeds and green wellingtons, flat hats and shooting-sticks, looking frightfully conspicuous and trying to get enough mud on their gumboots to establish their field credibility. All the women with brassy hair piled up on fancy combs, and the men sporting their Italian leatherware – enough Gucci binocular cases for a weekend at Newmarket.

'There were quite a few genuine country people – county, rather: you could tell them by the way they'd dressed up for the neighbours, all in couples; tweeds and twinsets or kaftans and grey flannel, depending on who had brought whom. Wiston strode right through the middle of the crowd, making loud remarks about "Dealers dealing in deal," while I tried to catch him up and keep a look out for the demon driver.

'The house itself was a nice double-fronted Georgian affair, stuccoed all over and painted white. It would have fetched a good price itself if it came up on the open market. Nice flight of stairs leading up to the door, and up and in we went, well ahead of the ruck. Met at the door by the auctioneer's touts, and sent upstairs to take a look at the goodies. They had everything set out in a long gallery on the first floor – rather an unusual thing to find in a house of that vintage – but the goods were just what you'd expect. Wiston grabbed a catalogue and went up and down with his nose to the piles of assorted lots, marking off items with a pencil and beckoning me over whenever anything caught his eye. All put on for the benefit of the dealers, but nobody seemed to be taking much notice of the pantomime, and frankly I started to find it all a bit embarrassing. Nice as the house was, it wasn't exactly a Mentmore, and I felt I'd driven a long way for a rather thin entertainment.

'After about twenty minutes of this, by which time I was aching for a cup of coffee and looking around surreptitiously for the loo, Wiston called me over in great excitement, and showed me an old mirror he'd stumbled across. Apparently it had been withdrawn from the sale, but he managed to get the family's agent to put it back in, though he refused to make them a private offer. The mirror was odd, and very old (much older than its frame) and metal, not glass: a copper plate silvered over. Wiston turned it round and tapped it (scattering showers of dust from the wormholes in the frame), scratched it with his fingernail and pronounced it, *sotto voce*, to be sixteenth century, around the fifteen-eighties. I asked him if he thought it was English or foreign, but he only smiled and told me to wait and see.

'The rest of the crowd were getting excited over the furniture and paintings, nice enough in their way but nothing that would have you jumping around. I was still on the look-out for our man in the sports-car, and not paying too much attention to the other goings-on. I suspected that Wiston had found what he wanted, but what I couldn't understand was this: why didn't he buy it when they offered it to him? Eventually one of the clerks came round ringing a handbell, and we all filed down to the parlour. The dealers sat in a row at the front, the real people in the middle, and Wiston and I at the back, on two of those village-hall chairs with canvas seats on tubular frames that clip together in rows. Wiston kept his head down and scribbled in his catalogue – no faces in mirrors this time, as it wasn't illustrated – while I played games deciding who would bid for what, and how high they would go, and concentrated on not catching the auctioneer's eye.'

The auctioneer had set up his pulpit against the longer wall of the room, and there were only a bare half-dozen rows of seats, so Born had a good view of the proceedings. There was no one he could identify as the driver of the sports-car, so he gave up looking and paid attention to the bidding.

The lots were fairly small, and the bidding went up in fives and tens, quite fast at first until the dealers found their level, and then sporadically in jerks as the other buyers – Born began to think of them as the congregation – put up their hands or waved their catalogues. The dealers bid on the nod, or with one finger raised.

Wiston had decided to buy Born a Hogarth print as a souvenir, before the mirror came up for sale, and took the bidding up to twenty pounds before a tenacious woman in the front row let him go: when it was knocked down to him, the other dealers turned and glowered, as if he had interrupted them at a private function. In retaliation, Wiston pushed up the bidding on another couple of items, one of which was knocked down to a county lady at a price well above its real value. Born tried the same trick a moment later, and nearly found himself landed with a porcelain ewer with a crack in the side: two or three of the dealers jeered audibly, and Wiston patted his sleeve. Domestic items, crockery, job lots of books and ledgers, the best of the furniture and paintings, the poorer ones going for the value of the glass and the frames. There was a pause while the auctioneer filled his glass with water and took a long draught.

'Washing the worm-dust away,' murmured Wiston. 'And my lot's coming up now.' The auctioneer cleared his throat.

'Lot seventy-five, a valuable antique mirror, silver-plated on to copper, in a carved pearwood frame. Late eighteenth century, restored to the list of items in the sale by the request of a member of the audience.' He nodded towards Wiston, who swore under his breath.

*Pantomime*, thought Born, *sheer pantomime*, and waited.

The assistant held it up, caught a beam of light from the window in the tarnished surface and played it like a jet of water across the room. The light, a grey light, fell on Wiston's face. The auctioneer fumbled under his lectern and pulled out an envelope, tore it open, drew out a card and read what was written on it. His eyebrows went up: he put on his spectacles and read it again: a dealer laughed in the front row.

'I have a bid here in writing for eight hundred pounds,' said the auctioneer. 'Somebody knows more than we do.' Wiston tapped Born sharply on the thigh with his catalogue, and pointed to a note he had scribbed: *Bid for me: – take it up to a thousand and then leave it to me.* Born nodded.

'I'll take it up from there in fifties,' said the auctioneer.

Born raised his catalogue.

'Eight hundred and fifty.' There was a movement in the corner of the room.

'Nine hundred.'

Another laugh from the dealers.

'Quite, please. Any advance on nine hundred pounds?'

Born raised his catalogue again.

'Nine hundred and fifty. We have a sportsman here.' No laughter from the dealers, but a titter from one of the county ladies. Another movement from the corner.

'Can I have that again, sir?'

The motion, more pronounced. Born did not dare to turn his head. The auctioneer took another sip of water.

'One thousand pounds.'

'At this moment Wiston gave me a nudge in the ribs, and put up his hand. Do you know, I almost started bidding against him. The two of them took it up to fifteen hundred, and Wiston was shaking in his seat. I still couldn't see who it was in the corner; if it wasn't the man in the sports-car . . . well, it was, there's no doubt at all. But he hadn't had a chance to get near the mirror before the sale – unless he was the one who had it withdrawn in the first place.'

'Fifteen hundred and fifty pounds. Any advance on fifteen fifty? Is anyone going to offer me one thousand and six hundred pounds for this elegant silver-plated mirror?' The hammer came down. 'Sold to the gentleman in the corner of the room for one thousand, five hundred and fifty pounds.'

'I could feel Wiston trembling through my chair: he had his head in his hands, his elbows on his knees, and he was shaking all over. He got up and I followed him, out of the auction-room, out of the house, and down the drive to where we had parked the car. I did not say a word. We stood there for five minutes or more, with Wiston grinding a hole in the gravel with his heel, as if he wanted to bury something there. I don't know how we missed the sports-car driver – he must have slipped out of the other door and come round the back of the house: all we heard was a roar of wheels, and he belted past us and out on to the road, no stopping, no signalling. I wanted to go after him, have a proper car chase, but Wiston wouldn't get into the car, just stood staring after him until I took him by the elbow and steered him back into the sale-room, where he picked up the Hogarth print and I bought a nice little drawing by Munnings, or school of, which I hoped would cheer him up. Then off on the open road, to find a place for a picnic.

# Chapter 6

Churchyards are good places for confidences, as the chances of being overheard, except by the occasional preoccupied mourner, are slight; Wiston felt also that a churchyard, after his defeat in the saleroom, was the only place likely to produce any appetite at all. How different, he thought, from the sterile cheerfulness of a municipal park, or even the inanities of a village green with its cricket pitch dry and grassless, its swings and slides all battered out of shape, paint chipped off and bearings wrenched by ruffians, is the well-kept tranquillity of a plot of uneven ground, with the occasional carved headstone displaying a rarer art than that of the local mason, and the pots of wilting anemones from the florist's overgrown with docks and nettles, creeping up from where the sexton's rotary mower had not reached. The sexton, he noticed, had left his scythe to rust against the wall of the boiler-house beside the vestry, with the sort of innocent symbolism that pleased a jaded eye.

Born's response to this elegy was a snort: he was hungry and wanted his lunch, so he wandered off around the graves to look at the inscriptions, leaving Wiston to carry the hamper up from the car, which stood by the wall looking like an undertaker's limousine left over from a funeral. Yews with scarlet berries leant over the bonnet, and bees were crawling over the hot black paintwork, drinking the drops of rainwater dripped from the trees.

'We'll lay the table here,' called Wiston, and spread a cloth over a flat-topped tomb. Born sauntered back, twisting a dandelion stem between his fingers.

'Let's hope we're out of sight of the vicarage,' he said. Wiston gave him a corkscrew and he opened a bottle of wine – one he recognized from the batch that Wiston had fetched the last time they ate together.

'I'm sorry you had that disappointment over the mirror,' said Born, still baffled by the whole affair. 'I must say I was put off my stride by that opening bid.'

*Understatement suits Born well,* thought Wiston: *you cannot tell if he is playing down the matter, or if he simply has not understood enough about what's going on to get excited or worried about it, let alone frightened. Almost like bravery, only without the element of choice.*

'I'm glad you didn't mind taking over the bidding – what if I'd left you in the lurch, holding a bit of brass in a wormeaten frame and a thousand-pound bill to pay?'

Born was frowning, and did not answer the question.

'He didn't want you to have it, did he? It wasn't as if he wanted it for himself. He knew you were after it, and he stopped you getting it, isn't that right?'

'You really think someone came all that way to stop me buying a mirror?'

Born thought for a moment.

'Yes. Yes, I do.'

Wiston laughed, and bit into a hard-boiled egg, dropping crumbs of yolk on to the grave-top. He pinched up some salt and licked it from his fingertips.

'And why should he want to do that?'

But Born had started on his lunch, and lost interest in the matter: he had found an answer that solved the problem, or part of it, and was happy to leave it at that. Wiston divided the rest of the food and poured out the wine into glasses – paper cups at a picnic being, to his mind, an abomination of desolation – and ate what he could with a pretence of an appetite. *I don't believe in keeping a man from his victuals,* he thought, *however much he wants to play at question and answer. The demon driver, wasn't that his phrase, or am I mind-reading?* Although he was enjoying their picnic, and liked Born's fine way of stripping off an eggshell with his teeth, Wiston felt he had chosen the wrong spot: he had not thought that the presence of so many graves would have affected his imagination as it did: it was as much as he could do to keep his mind on the food and away from the corruption around them.

'Let's take a look at that print you bought me,' said Born, when they had done with the cold tongue and hard-boiled eggs, and had moved on to oranges, chocolate and a thermos of coffee.

Wiston unwrapped the print, which he had kept with him. It was a Hogarth illustration to Samuel Butler's *Hudibras,* and showed Hudibras himself in the house of Sidrophel the magician, with the Puritan hero beating up the old soothsayer below the mummified crocodiles that hung from the ceiling, and scattering piles of papers with magical inscriptions across the table and on to the floor.

'Isn't it ugly?' said Born. 'The whole thing, I mean, not just the faces. There's something wrong with the way they're placed, with the disposition . . . There should be one more, just there –' and he jabbed his finger at a spot in the foreground, '– and that would balance the rest.

Don't you feel that, too?'

'I'm sorry you don't like it. It cost me twenty pounds.'

'Oh, I do like it.'

'Because it's ugly?'

'I don't know . . . perhaps it reminds me of something . . .'

Wiston turned it over, and pointed to the back. There were two couplets, written in an italic hand.

*Kelly did all his feats upon*
*The devil's looking-glass, a stone*
*Where playing with him at bo-peep*
*He solved all problems ne'er so deep.*

Born read the lines aloud.

'They're from the poem, aren't they?' Born was a subtle paleographer, and knew when not to ask questions. The ink was fresh on the paper, but the paper was two hundred years old.

'Who was Kelly?'

'Ah, Kelly, has anybody here seen Kelly? You mean to say you haven't ever come across Dee and Kelly in your wide and voluminous readings?'

'Dr John Dee the magician?'

'And Edward Kelly the soothsayer. Died of a fall from a window, and serve him right. Biggest fraud in Elizabethan England. Though he'd find some competition today. But Dee a magician, a mere conjuror? No, Dee was a scholar, an astronomer, navigator, cartographer, as well as being an astrologer and a crystal-gazer, and a Welshman like your friend, Master Thomas. Adviser to the Crown, owner of one of the largest private libraries in Europe, collector of rarities from the New World, and writer of some interesting diaries which might be worth your attention. All in the Western Manuscripts collection of the British Library.'

'You sound as if you're setting me up with the makings of a research project.'

Wiston rolled up the print, slid it into a cardboard tube and gave it to Born.

'With my compliments,' he said. 'Now tell me, how is your own work going? I forgot to ask you that the other night.'

'Coming along slowly as usual. I've been rather held up for the last week or two, waiting for some microfilms from a library in the States. You know the way it is.'

'Leaving you with plenty of time for parapsychological sessions with dungeon-master Thomas, with his ping-pong balls and his microphones?'

'And time to come to country auctions and chauffeur my friends around.'

'How nice for all of us.'

Wiston leaned back against an upright headstone, and felt the coolness coming through his hair where it was beginning to thin. Born, too, leaned back on his elbows, and turned his face to the sun, until all Wiston could see of it was the hollows of his nostrils and the dark stubble under his chin. The sun warmed them, and the wind brought them the heavy smell of petroleum vapour from the tank beside the boiler-house. Born took a cigarette out of a packet and lit it. *His nerves aren't as steady as they were this morning*, thought Wiston, *when he nearly bought a mirror for a thousand pounds. But he likes the Hogarth, and I shall grow to like the Munnings, too. I'll hang it over the bath.*

'How much work is there to be done on the Doctor Dee papers?'

'They all need editing, of course. Nobody's touched them since Meric Casaubon printed the second part of the diary in the sixteen-fifties.'

'I rather fancy taking it on.'

'Well, you won't have much trouble with the handwriting. Not where it's in Latin or English, at any rate.'

'What's the rest of it written in?'

'Some of it appears to be in a sort of debased or phonetically transcribed Bohemian – they went to Prague, you know, and the whole book is essentially a travel diary – but some of it, most of the incantations, for instance, is in some outlandish Babel dialect, worked out by plotting lines on to a chart of random letters arranged in squares. In the print, if you remember, one of Sidrophel's papers has a diagram of a similar kind, with a diamond in a square in a diamond in a square and so on to the edges of the paper, like a child's fortune-teller.'

'Why has no one edited it?'

'Well, you can imagine the cranks it attracted, from Aleister Crowley onwards and backwards. But it's an important piece of work.'

'What do you find interesting about it, then?'

Wiston let out a long breath, and uncrossed his fingers.

'Dee had the best scientific apparatus obtainable at the time: a mind trained in mathematics and logic. His preface to Euclid remained unchallenged for two hundred years; he knew Francis Drake and Giordano Bruno, and corresponded with most of the learned men of Europe, yet he was taken in, taken in by a confidence trickster whose ears had been cropped in the pillory, who dragged him away from Mortlake and his library, led him a dance around the courts of Prague and Cracow, and sent him back in disgrace, broken, under accusation of treachery and witchcraft, so that he went in fear of his life, selling off his books for a square meal, and dying poor, old, alone, out of his time.'

'Out of his time indeed,' said Born, agreeing.

'Who isn't? Was I born for an age of machines and computers? Were you?'

'Oh, I think so,' said Born. 'But Kelly died too?'

'Yes, in Prague: he jumped out of a window in the Hradschin Palace, fell into a ditch and broke his legs.'

'Tell me about the devil's looking-glass.'

'It was – it is – a mirror, a stone mirror, made of obsidian, Aztec, brought over from Mexico by the Conquistadores. Given to Doctor Dee by someone who thought he'd find a use for it.'

'And did he?'

'He couldn't use it himself, as he had not "studied" – that was his phrase – so he gave it to Kelly, and Kelly saw all sorts of things in it, or so he said, and Dee wrote them all down in the diary. Dee thought he saw angels, but Kelly knew better.'

'So Dee forced Kelly to use the stone?'

*Well done, my pupil,* thought Wiston, *intelligently said.*

'Why should he?' *The innocent questioner never fails.*

'Oh, I don't know. I always feel that there's some sort of contract involved in these matters. One to play the sorcerer and the other the apprentice. And it isn't always the sorcerer who has to face . . .'

'Aha! I see! You're being coerced by Magister Thomas, are you? Held in captivity to see his visions for him? Bound to your couch, deafened and blinded until you come up with some satisfactory hallucinations? Are you a party to his Faustian ambitions?'

'One does feel . . . obliged to present him with something. It's so disappointing when nothing happens.'

'Disappointing for him? Is that the true spirit of scientific detachment? Is that what all those white coats and gleaming gadgets are for, all those masked laboratory technicians, to hide the fact that someone's emotions are involved? This would seem to be a most dangerous state of affairs.'

Born nodded. Wiston reached out and caught his

elbow, and continued.

'Are you sure he's keeping his own emotions out of it? Perhaps he likes watching people lying defenceless on couches until he gives them the order to get up, and tying them into place with electrical wiring. What does he do when you're deaf and blind, with those absurd things over your eyes? Pull faces?'

Wiston felt tempted to make other suggestions, unworthy ones, to go crudely into details of obsessive fantasies – and were they his own, or those of some imaginary person?

'The thought had crossed my mind. But then, we're not exactly operating under laboratory conditions. For a start, it's all done in my room, and all he has to do is make up the couch, plug in the apparatus, change the light-bulb –'

'The bulb?'

'Sometimes we use a red light – no, don't laugh, it's perfectly serious, it isn't a joke. It's supposed to make the subject –'

'You?'

'Yes, me – more relaxed, tranquil, open to suggestion.'

Wiston lay flat on his back in a fit of laughter, and rapped his head on the gravestone. Born was laughing, too.

'You seem to find this all terribly funny.'

'Well, what with the red lights, couches, soft music –'

'White noise, actually. Just a sort of hiss.'

'Like the serpent in the garden. It all sounds like a seduction scene in a very old movie.'

'Oh, you couldn't get more straight up and down than Thomas, come on now. He's got a wife and two kids.'

*And thereby hangs a tale,* thought Wiston, *a very long tale.*

'What a thought, though,' said Born.

'He's trying to get you enthralled. You're being turned

into a white mouse, a guinea-pig. And you know, as soon as you start coming up with the goods, you'll be indispensable. He won't be able to do without you. You'll be stuck on that couch for life.'

Born wiped the plates on a wisp of grass and put them back in the hamper.

Wiston went on.

'Now what was it he promised you? What did he offer? New insight into your personality? The secret of your soul? What it is that makes you tick? Or stops you ticking the way you'd like?'

Born shook his head.

'Believe me, it's a fraud. The oldest one in the book. The mystics did it, the Sufi, the gurus, the priests, the psychoanalysts: give me your mind, your soul, and I will show you their secrets, the secrets that drive the universe.'

Born shut the lid of the hamper and drove the wicker pin through the hasps that held it down, then swung the hamper up by its handles, and carried it down to the car. Wiston followed him.

'Then why is there only you? All the others have crowds of assistants. People queue up to be told they're psychic, or sensitive, or saintly, or whatever is the phrase of the moment. But here it's just the two of you. Which are you, Dee or Kelly? Hudibras or Sidrophel?'

'Perhaps I'm the one who was missing from the picture.'

They got into the car.

*No, you're not,* thought Wiston as they drove away, *and nor am I. I wonder . . .*

Born drove silently, gazing at the road without humour in his face, but Wiston allowed himself to smile. In spite of the disappointment, it had been a most enjoyable day.

## Chapter

# 7

Born did not write to his mother about the conversation in the churchyard, and he had little to say to her about his subsequent sessions with Thomas. But he made notes in the green notebook, leaving them in the drawer where Wiston found them.

The next session was on the Monday after the sale, in the evening after the library had closed. Born had spent the day with a tall folio in blind-stamped ecclesiastical calf, Casaubon's book on Dee, reading and taking notes. He found it as Wiston had said, a bewildering mixture of tongues and typefaces, with passages of narrative and dialogue – Dee's name marked with a capital delta – interspersed with pages of uncouth names and invocations, tables and charts of the names of angelic spirits. He signed the book out promptly at nine in the morning, as soon as the library was open: Wiston checked this later with the assistant librarian, a small round man whose thin beard gave him the look of an Egyptian priest.

'That was the first day he started coming in regularly, Dr Wiston. A sad piece of news. I see they're still flying the flag at half-mast. No, just the one volume at first, I can give you the class-mark if you like. Then he moved to some other printed works of the same period. They're listed in the ledger. Some of them hadn't been off the shelves since we last restored the bindings – and that would be four or five years ago.'

The smell of linseed oil and turpentine, cedarwood and lanolin, clung to Wiston's fingers after he had left the library. He felt he had just paid a visit to the embalmers, and that the mummifying ointment that preserved the leather was originally made to keep the readers themselves from corruption. He remembered how the two trades went together, how the library at Alexandria had burned down, and how the books torn up by the embalmers for wrappings and mummy-cases had preserved the texts for the resurrection-men, the restorers in their laboratories, to unpeel and piece together. *The mortuary odours and relentless recording of librarians mark their succession to the ancient priesthood,* thought Wiston: *they are older than the books among which they sit, and have an even older ritual than mine.*

Born was eating his supper off a plate balanced on his knees when Thomas came round to see him, and was reading through his notes. Thomas found the door open, and came in without knocking.

'Gives you indigestion, reading and eating together. You can't hope to concentrate with your mouth full, and we can't hold a séance if you've got the wind.'

'I like the way you're calling it a séance,' said Born, putting his plate down and slipping the green notebook into the desk drawer. 'You make it sound like table-rapping. Did anyone tell you you've got an aura?'

'My Auntie Myfanwy, up in the valley, used to tell me something of the sort,' said Thomas cheerfully, 'If I turn one way it's daffodil yellow, and if I turn the other –' he spun round on his heels – 'it's a rather pretty shade of leek green. Comes of being a Welshman, you understand.'

Born seemed to find this amusing: his trip to the country with Wiston had blown away the cobwebs and let in a little fresh air. One can get stale, sitting in libraries day after day, however well-lit and lofty, waiting for inspiration; and a jaunt around the villages, in Wiston's opinion, did much to refresh the mind. It was a pity the old Victorian tradition of reading-parties in the Lakes had fallen into decline: a conjunction of sound minds and healthy bodies, clear air and high altitude always brought good results. Wiston would have liked to take Born walking in the hills, to find a high spot with a good view all round, where he could open his mind to its own capabilities. But it was too late now.

Thomas was explaining his terminology.

'No, my calling it a séance comes from spending the day in the Periodicals Library reading through the back-numbers of the psychical research magazines. All the way from spoon-bending and fortune-telling to the latest stuff on extrasensory perception and Psi theory. Quite intelligently written, as a matter of fact. I thought it would be all mediums and dotty old gentlemen in Hove, but they all seem to have decent credentials, and some of them are quite eminent in their own specializations.' *Thomas's tongue has a way round a polysyllable like a child licking a lollipop,* thought Born. *I'm getting as catty as Wiston, I must watch it.*

'Most of the stuff that interested me and had any relevance to our project was some of the Russian work on flash-cards, transference of images in hallucinatory states, or under Ganzfeld conditions like the ones we've been producing. I'm wondering if we shouldn't be moving in that direction ourselves.'

'You mean you look at pictures and I try to guess what you're looking at.'

'Not quite as crude as that, not quite as conscious. There's no trying involved, you see: you just lie there while I go through the pictures, and you tell me afterwards if any images cross your mind. You write up your notes, I write up mine, then we check to see if there's any correlation.'

'How would you explain it if it does work? Surely you're not suggesting there's a spiritual force in operation?'

'You can call it what you like. I'm just interested in finding what's there, if anything, and trying to measure it.'

'You're expecting some sort of telepathic transmission?'

'That's the idea. I have a hunch we were getting there the other afternoon, when that magazine-picture came through.'

'Just coincidence, that we both happened to be thinking of it at the same moment.'

'Coincidences are precisely what I want to test. I want to see if we can get better at it, improve our technique. You see, most of these other experiments have been done by sifting through a fairly large population of subjects, and they've been so careful to maintain controls, they've hardly had time to practise the art itself.'

'So you think mind-reading is something you can learn?'

'Not in the vulgar sense – no, it will just be picking up a set of signals, like a radio-ham with a directional aerial, tuning in to the strongest frequencies.'

'So why doesn't this happen all the time?'

'Too much interference. You haven't tuned your receiver.'

'So the Ganzfeld . . .'

'– Acts as a filter, and also as an amplifier. There's not enough sensory input to block the signals, but not so little that the brain thinks the switches have been pulled, and throws a blue fit.'

'So what's the source of the signal?'

'Mental activity is the product of minute electrochemical changes in the cortex of the brain. Any electrical current produces a magnetic field which can be picked up by another conductor nearby.'

'So you're suggesting we should put our heads together?'

'There's plenty of wisdom in the old sayings if you know where to look for it. There's a Welsh proverb . . .'

'One of your Auntie Myfanwy's?'

Thomas cuffed him on the side of the head.

'All I mean is, there might be some chance that one brain – and remember we're talking about a physical object, a machine – might pick up and amplify the side-effects of another brain's thought, the electrical resonances if you like, and amplify them. Something you couldn't hope to do with a mechanical reading.'

'So it's like tapping a phone by wrapping a wire round the cable?'

'Just that. And if you think about it, it would be a fairly obvious survival technique for creatures living in a herd.'

'So you all go astray together?'

'A panicking response is bound to give a stronger signal than a calm reaction, so yes, if my thesis is correct, that would follow.'

'And certain individuals might find they had greater powers of influence than others, just by the amount of electrical energy they could project.'

'It isn't beyond the realms of possibility. No, the point is, it should be something you can train yourself to do.

Take the adrenalin response, for instance . . .'

Thomas brought his face close to Born's.

'Look at my eyes, look at the pupils.'

Born looked at Thomas's eyes, noticing for the first time that the pupils were green, true green, without a trace of blue or brown. The two eyes swam together as his own went out of focus, then separated into four, then back to one: a cyclopean Thomas stared from the middle of a ring of hair.

'You're too close.' Thomas moved back a little, and held his breath. His cheeks went red and his chest began to heave.

'Now what's happening?'

'You look as if you're having a stroke.'

'No, you idiot, look at my pupils.'

Born focused on the pupil of Thomas's left eye: the green fringe of the iris was opening and closing over the black hole of the pupil like the mouth of a sea-anemone. He saw his own face, reflected and inverted, balanced over the mouth, and draw back sharply.

'You're making them dilate.'

'Exactly. And it's supposed to be an automatic response to changes of light intensity. But it's also linked to the adrenalin response, so that when you hear a snarl from the back of the cave –' – Thomas drew back his lips and growled – 'your pupils widen and let in enough light for you to see that sabre-toothed tiger in the back there. And you hop it. But you can do it voluntarily, if you will yourself to feel the right sensations.'

'How do you bring it on?' Born squatted back on his heels, and the soles of his shoes squeaked on the floor.

'I don't know. It's something I found out how to do when I was a kid, in front of the bathroom mirror. Like wiggling your ears. You sort of tighten your chest, hold your breath, try to feel dizzy, and there you are. I can't explain it if you've never done it.'

'I have.'

'Then why the hell didn't you say so?'

'I wanted to hear you put it into words.'

'Well, I hope you're enlightened.'

'You described it exactly as I would have done.'

'Good, that's an advantage. Do you know,' said Thomas, with self-satisfaction, 'I feel we're beginning to build up quite a rapport.'

Born took his plate to the kitchen and washed it under the tap. When he came back, Thomas was searching along the shelves, pulling out any illustrated books he could find, thumbing them through and putting them back where they came from.

'What we need,' he said without turning round, 'is something with pictures that you haven't seen before, that we can use until I can get some flashcards.'

'Oh, I wouldn't bother with flashcards, not for the time being,' said Born. 'If I can find a book or a magazine I haven't read, wouldn't that do?'

'It might, if the pictures were fairly simple. Something with a good clear outline and a shape you could easily recognize.'

'This might be what we're looking for. I haven't opened it.' Born gave Thomas the buff manila envelope with Wiston's name on it. The seal was intact.

'What have you got there?'

'It's an exhibition catalogue Wiston gave me when I went to dinner.' Born, discreet, had not mentioned the Saturday excursion, nor would he.

'Sounds ideal. Did he have a lot of that sort of thing?'

'Oh, mountains of the stuff. Calls it his pornography, reads it in bed.'

'Well, whatever turns you on. Can I open it?'

'Yes, open it, but don't show it to me.'

'You sure you haven't seen it?'

'Cross my heart.'

Thomas ripped open the flap of the envelope and slid out the contents, while Born turned his back and held his hands, quite unnecessarily, over his eyes.

'It's all right, you can turn round,' said Thomas. 'Looks just what we need. It'll do us for a day or two at least.'

He put the catalogue down on the desk, and went to help Born fit the covers to his eyes and ears and lie down on the couch.

'Good photographs, too,' he said, waiting for some sign of recognition.

Born, sightless and deaf, his eyes capped and bulbous, lay on the couch without replying. Thomas studied the lines on his face for signs of duplicity, but found none. Born had not seen the pictures in the catalogue, Thomas was sure, but then, why should Wiston have given it to him in the first place? Born was wondering this too, as he lay there in the semi-darkness and imperfect silence. He tried to listen for the turning of the pages, but, beyond the hissing of the headphones, he could hear nothing.

# Chapter 8

Thomas opened the stiff covers of the catalogue, making as little noise as he could. His first shock was that the text was in Italian, incomprehensible to him; his second, the variety and complexity of the illustrations, of woodcuts from old books, early botanical drawings, strange alchemical diagrams of pointed stars with letters and black rays, mystical images of monochords and celestial harmonies, the proportions of the universe and the orders of creation. Dragons, lizards, one-legged men sheltering from the sun below a single huge foot; monsters of the Antipodes and the Americas crowded the pages; and alembics and bolt-heads, stills and furnaces for transmuting metals stood out from them like items on shelves, like the majolica jars of drugs in an apothecary's shop. The jars were there, too, with their metallic glazes shining like the substances they held, plump as Paracelsus (shown in a woodcut) or narrow-waisted like witches in a coven. Thomas puzzled out their dates and sources, and the names of the subjects, but some words escaped him, and blocked his mind from deciphering the rest.

*From Magic to Science under the Medici* – that must roughly translate the title; and the cover, with a grandly-inscribed Seal of Solomon in black against green, encouraged the magical rather than the scientific interpretation. Thomas thumbed through the catalogue again, and the impression was stronger: science, true science, had been shuffled to the back, behind all the claptrap about witchcraft and astrology, alchemy and necromancy. Even the astrolabes and backstaffs, by their juxtaposition with zodiacal charts and tables of nativity, were forced into a false conjunction with magic; and Galileo's telescope, which should have had pride of place in the exhibition as the image of the new clear-sightedness, was tucked away in an appendix as being out of its time, untypical of the spirit of the age.

Thomas flicked through the book again: his first impression, that all the items were from Italian collections, was a wrong one. German, Austrian, French and Spanish museums had given up their treasures, and cases had been filled with spoils returned from Russia and America. Some items from Florence itself, mottled by the floodwaters, seemed older and more travel-worn than those from more remote museums. Thomas stared at one picture after another, then looked up at Born on the couch, lying beneath the red bulb like a plate developing in a darkroom, flattened out by the crimson light and the sharp-edged shadows into something featureless and disturbing, only the eyes clearly visible, staring from his face like the eyes of an Aztec figure.

And here was a mirror, the same unmistakable shape of a disk with a handle that he had seen in the planetary tables denoting Venus, only the handle was without a cross-piece. It had been distorted by the camera's foreshortening into a black flattened oval with a blunt projection and one hole drilled for a cord.

*'Specchio di ossidiana, realizzato in Messico nel 400, già di proprietà del Dott. John Dee, mago elisabettiano, e da lui usato per profetizzare il futuro. Oggi esposto nel British Museum.'* Thomas turned the page, then went back to the picture of the mirror. The surface, even in the photograph, was bright, as bright as anything so black could be. *Ossidiana* would be obsidian, a naturally-occurring volcanic glass that took a fine polish. Oddly, on the next page the image was reversed, a white wax disc on a black background, not smooth like the mirror but matt, discoloured, and carved or moulded with the same design as that on the cover of the book, a star of interlocking points, with figures and letters in some alphabet he could not read. If he could decipher the words in the centre . . . but his eyes wandered back to the mirror on the opposite page, the black disk against the white.

If Born picked anything up, it would be one or both of these, Thomas was sure. But other images were too complex, he would have to bring in his flashcards and stare at them one by one – cat, tree, house, ace of hearts, sun – and see if the images would project themselves into Born's mind. Thomas had moments of increasing scepticism, he told Wiston later, when he felt that the chances of the experiment working were diminishing to zero; and the phrases from the journals did not help at all.

'Some of them were quite obviously written by cranks,' Thomas told Wiston. 'You know the sort of nonsense: colour recognition by touch, the kind of thing the Russians were doing in the thirties.'

'It was just the same four hundred years ago. All they wanted to look at were the freaks, the variations from the norm, before they had done any systematic classification.'

Thomas had come to return the catalogue.

'You should never have lent it to him. It was the root of

all the trouble. You should have stuck to those sale-room pamphlets, if you wanted to give him something to look at.'

It was the first time he had accused Wiston, even indirectly, of any malign intention, but in the days after Born's death it was something he harped upon increasingly.

'I had no idea you'd be using them for your sessions,' Wiston had said. 'I thought flashcards were the order of the day.'

'You're quite right. I should have stuck to them. It's the same freak-show fallacy in operation. I hated that catalogue, and do you know why? It showed that same lack of systematic observation, the same bad methods we were using towards the end.'

Wiston stroked the catalogue, as if to console it.

'Don't be too hard on them. They had named all the stars they could see, and they had discovered algebra and the logarithmic tables. They had charted the coasts and worked out how to find the longitude, roughly at least. They were starting to question Aristotle, and were beginning to have doubts about astrology and alchemy. And the best logical weapon they had, Occam's razor, was another two centuries older than that. From Roger Bacon to Francis Bacon was a long time, time for plenty of hard thinking. And the Neoplatonists –'

Thomas stamped his foot: evidently, he had no sympathy with Neoplatonism. Wiston felt sorry for him.

'The funny thing is, if you'd read that paper of yours in 1582, they'd have elected you to a professorial chair.'

'Burnt me at the stake, more likely,' grunted Thomas, and walked away with his shoulders hunched.

*No*, thought Wiston, *that's what they'd do today*.

But now Thomas was sitting over the same catalogue, staring diligently at a black disk foreshortened on a white page, and a white circle on black, his eyes switching from one to the other, and his eyelids growing heavy. He fell asleep as he sat, leaning forward in his chair, until he woke to a shaking of his shoulder, and a vision from a nightmare: a face with bulbous staring eyes six inches from his own, eyes like hard-boiled eggs, like the eyes of a blind Chinese sage in an ivory carving, lidless, expressionless, eyes like – like precisely what they were, halved ping-pong balls embedded in a friendly, grinning face. Born's face, and Born was shaking his shoulder.

'I knew that would give you a shock,' said Born. 'I thought you'd nodded off.' He had unhitched himself from the white-noise generator, and the headphones were hissing quietly on the couch.

'Whatever made you get up?' Thomas shut the catalogue and slid it into its envelope, almost as a reflex action.

'I got up,' said Born, peeling the shells from his eyes, 'for a very interesting reason.' He leaned across the table and stared at Thomas, who moved backwards in his chair.

'And what might that have been?'

'The pictures stopped coming through.'

'It worked, then?'

'Oh, yes, it worked. It worked, all right. I'll say it worked. It worked so well that when the pictures stopped, I thought to myself, the lazy beggar, he's gone to sleep. So I came over and woke you up. I hoped I'd give you a scare.'

'You certainly did that,' said Thomas, rubbing his forehead. 'Now tell me about the pictures.'

'You don't want me to write it down and send it on a postcard?'

'No I bloody don't.' Thomas thumped both fists on the table.

'What I saw was this. I was daydreaming in the usual way, and the sound didn't seem as loud as before. There was more red in the light, which made it easier to concentrate: my eyes weren't straining all the time. I felt I was focusing at infinity, at a point beyond infinity, and then, at no particular distance away, things started floating by. Flat objects, with no depth or dimension, and . . . they took away my own sense of size, of relative position. They were perfectly clear, not blurred or hazy, but flat, as if there were nothing, could be nothing behind them.'

Thomas put a pencil into his hand, and gave him a sheet of paper, folded in half.

'Draw them for me.'

Born drew, hesitantly at first, feeling the moistness of the end where Thomas had chewed the pencil. *Graphite is a conductor*, he thought; *what if a current should pass down my fingers and into the paper?* The pencil marked a black line like a scorch, charred into the white sheet like the ink into the back of the Hogarth print. The verses came into his head again as his hand traced outlines on the page, and filled them in with roughly scribbled shading. Thomas bent his head over the desk.

'I'm not going to comment,' he said. 'Just draw them in the order they came into your head.'

Born continued to scribble, waisted shapes like the bodies of wasps, beaked figures and twisted curves like dragons, like waves. Thomas nodded over them.

'The last two are the easiest to draw.'

With a turn of the wrist he drew a circle, and began to fill it in.

'Giotto couldn't have done better.' He rounded out the roughnesses in the contour, and continued his shading, more and more heavily, until the point of the pencil had worn down and the black disk on the page had a dull shine to it, a darkly reflective surface. Thomas showed it to Wiston much later, who noted how deeply the pencil had indented the paper and how dense was the layer of graphite. But now Thomas looked, and waited, and did not say a word.

Born stared at the diagram. Then he drew a tentative outline, a little promontory, a basalt peninsula. He began to shade it solidly in, then stopped, licked his finger and rubbed a spot on the middle of the projection.

'It isn't so dark there.'

Thomas watched.

Born drew another circle, almost the same, but without the shading, or the mark at the side. He stared at it, then drew lines from side to side, making a pentagram, a Seal of Solomon. He had begun to scribble some letters at the points when Thomas grabbed his wrist.

'You saw that. You saw that on the cover.'

'What?'

'That's the diagram on the cover of the book. Don't cheat, it's too important.'

Born thrust out his lower lip in a pout, the image of a sulking child.

'I'm not cheating. That's what I saw. And I never looked at the cover. He only showed me the back before he put it into the envelope.'

If this was deception, it was too transparent for Thomas to take it seriously.

'You saw it all in black and white?'

'Yes, but not absolutely: the black was reddish and the white was yellowish, but that could have been due to the light.'

'We could try a different bulb. But you're absolutely certain there was no depth to them, the images?'

'None at all, completely flat, like something projected

on to a screen. Like shadows.'

'You couldn't tell, for instance, whether this was a plate or a ball, flat or spherical?'

'I've no idea. If you hadn't nodded off just then . . .'

'How could you tell I had?'

'Just like I said, the images stopped, as if you had switched them off. It made me cross, to tell you the truth. The last one, and the one before the last, those two disks, were coming through clearest of all. I would say it was a plate, though, the black one, judging by the hole in the handle, if it was a handle.'

'You don't want to try it again? See if it comes through better?'

'No, I'd rather not. Will you take a turn on the couch?'

Thomas shook his head violently. *So he's the sorcerer*, thought Born, *and I'm the apprentice. But let's see if we can't turn the tables*. He said aloud:

'Don't want to be your own guinea-pig, then? Sensible man. Don't go meddling in the realms of darkness. Next time you decide to take a nap, though, you'd better warn me: I don't want to eavesdrop on your fantasies.'

# Chapter 9

Wiston met Born in the avenue, heading for the library.

'We could go through the garden, don't you think, and take a turn around the Roundabout?' This was the name the Fellows gave to the perimeter path encircling the big lawn, the Mount of Olives, the patch of rough grass called the Wilderness, and the orchard, known from earliest times by the name of Paradise.

Born fell into step with Wiston, and they crossed the road together. Wiston opened the high wrought-iron gate into the garden and let Born through, followed him and clanged it shut behind them. A newly-planted row of plane-trees led to a freshly-dug pond, but they avoided these novelties and turned leftward by the variegated beech, the medlar and the Siberian crab-apple. The roses were in full bloom around the sundial, but they did not stop to admire them.

There was some hard fruit on the medlar, and a few green berries on the mulberry, only the odd one turning to red under a leaf: the cloudy weather had delayed the season, and left the fruit unripe. Wiston stretched up and picked the few ripe berries within reach, and gave them to Born, who ate them greedily, the red juice staining his fingers. The juice was acid, and made his teeth feel raw about the roots, stripped of enamel.

'How have your hallucinations been progressing?'

'Oh, I've reached the first two stage of madness, seeing things and talking to myself.'

'So long as you haven't started growing hairs on the palms of your hands – that's the third sign,' said Wiston. Born turned up his palm. 'Or looking for them – that's the fourth.'

Born sucked at the mulberry stains on his fingers, but they would not come off. Wiston looked into the branches, but there were no more berries to be seen. He clasped his hands behind his back and walked on, reminiscing.

'I often wonder, what with these short academic generations, high turnover, short tenure and so forth, how the older dons must seem to you. There's only a difference in age between us of – what, fifteen years? – yet when I think of men now in their middle fifties, and remember how old and odd they seemed when I was your age . . .'He led Born along the path and under the laburnum, turning with the sun and going clockwise around the garden. 'I remember one of the old guard, he would have been in his sixties now, coming round this very path, the opposite way to us –'

'Widdershins, you mean.'

'– And wondering what it would be like to get as thoroughly crabbed, eccentric and peculiar, as wild-haired and fantastical-looking. He was obsession personified. I have his rooms now, and his mirror, the little one let into the panel. He carved the frame around it himself, I believe. Very skilful in many ways, but quite, quite mad. He used to carry that mirror about with him, you know, like Ibsen with his vanity-glass in his top hat, only he kept it in his pocket. Perfectly understandable in a woman, quite commonplace I believe, so why should it seem so odd in a man? I often think we are as strange in our conformities as any nonconformist is in his. Look at that box-tree, now –'

Startled, Born turned and stared, as if it might conceal some singularly mad old don.

'You see the way the top has been broken in? It used to have a nice, smooth shape like an upturned pudding-basin until a dozen undergraduate hearties threw some poor individual into its upper branches to celebrate his coming-of-age. Perfectly normal behaviour. They didn't even get sent down.'

The path turned again, and they were facing the pond at the end of the avenue, surrounded by its octagon of trees.

'The old mad Fellow and I talked in here once or twice: he had some strong opinions about colour-combinations in herbaceous borders and was cursing at a bed of salvias – why he didn't pull them up and have done with it, I can't imagine. Then he took out the mirror and stared at himself in it, to check if he was still there, I suppose. He wasn't all there, of course, but I couldn't tell him that. Then he started muttering about how he had an obsession, I had an obsession, and how we were the lucky ones . . . then off he ran, yelling at some poor innocent sunbather. He did go mad, not just eccentric but stark, staring mad, that very night, in the garden, with the mirror in his hand. I had come out again after dinner to take a breath of air, and he was standing on the spot where they've dug the pond, with the full moon behind him, shining the light into his face. Then as he tilted the mirror down . . . he saw . . .'

'What did he see?'

'What did he see? He saw his face, of course. That's what you see if you look into mirrors.'

'Was it . . . so bad?'

'Under certain conditions, and unprotected . . .'

'What do you mean? No magic circle?'

They walked to the edge of the pond where the newly-laid turf was still showing dark earth at the edges, and a tuft of plastic sheeting, sealing the bottom of the pond, stuck up like black seaweed at the margin.

'You tell me, you're the one who reads the books. Since you've been looking at some manuscripts recently, you can tell me what you think of this.'

Wiston pulled a slip of paper from his pocket, and handed it to Born.

'Try and work out what it says, and then sing it to me.'

Born bent his head over the page: it was a single leaf, yellowed and fractured at the edges. It could have been four hundred years old, he thought, late sixteenth, early seventeenth-century. The writing was in secretary hand, the 'c's like 't's and the 's's long and flourishing, the capitals heavily swashed and ornamental. He counted along the line with one finger, reading what he could from the recognizable letters and working out the rest. The tune was written on a single stave above the words, and he hummed it under his breath.

'What is it?'

'It is a song from a masque. I'd date it around sixteen thirty-two to three. An Entertainment at Dering Castle, in Kent. This leaf comes from the Record Office in Maidstone. I suppose it ought to go back there.'

'Are you going to return it?'

'No.'

The daylight was bright, and the waters of the pond were quite still and, with their black plastic underlay, reflective, and, thought Wiston irrelevantly, mercifully free from goldfish. He could foresee a row looming up on the subject with the Junior Bursar. But now, he waited.

Born sang.

> *'By these Stygian waters shed*
> *From the fountains of the Ded*
> *I write my selfe in Life and Death*
> *Thy other-selfe thy shaddowe and thy Breath.'*

There was a figure standing on the opposite bank of the pond.

> *'When this Sprite is mixt with Aire*
> *And Proserpine has cutt my haire*
> *Yet do I bind my soule to bee*
> *The willing Bondsman of thy Arte and Thee.'*

Wiston's projecting vision, working out of place, had given him quite a turn. He banished the figure of the Fellow with the moon in his looking-glass from his mind's eye, and the further bank was empty.

Born had sung the verses in the thin high voice of one intoning a prayer or an incantation.

'I'm not sure of the scansion of the second line, last verse.'

'You were quite right: she is "Proserpine" to rhyme with "columbine"or "intertwine". Well done for getting the melody right first time.'

'And why "cutt my haire"?'

'To set your soul free from your body after death. Just one lock.' Wiston took a strand of Born's hair between his scissored fingers, and made a snipping motion. Born pulled away sharply, tugging a few hairs out by the roots. Wiston wound them round two fingers, and put his hand in his pocket.

'I thought that was Iris,' said Born.

'No, no, she only came for Dido. Dido was a special

case. She died before her time.'

They walked across the garden. Born was singing.

*'When I am laid, am laid in earth*
*May my wrongs create*
*No trouble, no trouble in . . . thy breast . . .'*

'Music by Henry Purcell, words by Nahum Tate,' said Wiston.

'Who wrote the music for the Entertainment?'

'The man who wrote the words, I would imagine.'

Born laughed. Wiston folded the paper and slipped it into his pocket.

'I must go back to the library.'

'I must go back into college.'

'I want to follow you.'

*Yes,* thought Wiston, *and if I tell you to, you will, two steps behind.*

He turned like a priest entering the ante-chapel after Mass, and made the gesture of dismissal, then went across the lawn towards the college and down the cathedral-avenue of trees, without turning back. Born watched him go, then went slowly across the garden and out at the wicket-gate.

# Chapter 10

'We'll try this time with a white light,' said Thomas at their next session.

'Why white?'

'I'm hoping to improve the contrast.'

'You make it sound like a television set.'

'If we can make the image black and white, instead of orange and yellow, the shapes ought to come through more clearly.'

'Yes, you're right. It's just that I'm not too keen on bare filament bulbs.'

'You won't see the filament with your blinkers on. It'll be just like looking at a pearl-coated lamp.'

Born lay down under the naked light and clamped the covers over his eyes to protect them from the scarring, twisted thread of incandescent metal. The ping-pong balls seemed to squint upward, malevolently.

'I bumped into Wiston today,' said Thomas. 'Looking very pleased with himself, he was.'

'Oh, yes?'

'He wanted to know how things were going.' Thomas

paused. Could Born see his face now, by projection, or tell its expression? The blind can judge the moods of others, and Born, in his pearly blinkers, was as sensitive as any blind man. 'He seems to know quite a bit about it. Wanted to find out some more, I think. He's asked me round to dinner.'

'Perhaps he wants to pick your brains.'

'Like he's picked yours, maybe.'

Born sat up, and pulled off one of the blinkers. It gave him a monstrous, disquieting look. His one free eye stared out at Thomas, who could not judge its expression.

'I've said practically nothing to him about it. Or to anyone else, for that matter. If you want to swear me under a vow of silence –'

'No, no, don't get me wrong. It's just that . . . I have the feeling we're on to . . .'

'Something bigger than the two of us?' Thomas, impervious as an anvil to cracks of this kind, wrinkled up his brows.

'I do wish you'd take that off, or put the other one back on. Makes you look like a bloody pirate.'

'A good, virtuous pirate, with a white eye-patch.'

'Where's your parrot, then? Fine pirate you'd make, with no bloody parrot.'

Born capped his other eye again, and lay obediently on the couch, while Thomas busied himself at the table, laying out the catalogue, his notebook and a little pile of cards. Born heard the fall of the cards quite clearly, and found that he had not properly fitted the headphones: one of them was a little awry, but he let it stay as it was.

'Actually, you might find the simplest thing is just to let the book fall open, and stare at one page for a while. See if anything comes through. Give me some time to adjust, though.'

'How long do you think you'll be needing?'

'Half an hour or so, if last time's anything to go by.'

Thomas sighed, and laid his watch on the table. He rested the catalogue upright on its spine, and let it fall open, then stared down at the page, and resisted the temptation to let his eyes lose their focus and blur the image. *Lo specchio . . . ossidiana . . . British Museum . . .* filtered through, and he let his eyes run lazily along the Italian text, and back over the picture of the mirror. Strange that Born had drawn it as a circle and not as an oval: as if the image had corrected itself before transmission. He let his mind manipulate the image, turning it over and visualizing it from the side, the back. Was the back polished, and did it show the same . . . But of course it did, he thought sharply, correcting himself, and turned the page.

'That's funny,' said Born from the couch. 'I had something coming through quite clearly until just a second ago.'

Thomas obediently turned the page back without trying to conceal the sound, and saw Born relax on the couch like a man settling down in his hotel room to watch a good late-night movie on the television at the foot of his bed. Thomas found it hard to concentrate on the image of the mirror, but whenever he took his attention away from the page and looked up, the blinded, deafened figure on the couch would stiffen, and only relax again when his attention returned. He began to feel like a puppet-master with his hand on the strings, and playfully twitched the page to watch Born flinch. He felt there was a line, a telegraph between them, carrying the signal across the room, with Born the obedient receiver. He stared again at the mirror, which even in the photograph had a dimly reflective surface, and let his perspective faculty – that tells the mind that a cycle-wheel seen from an oblique angle is truly round, not buckled out of shape – complete the mirror's circle and send it rolling across the room, the image of a flat black stone, accurately polished until you could see your face in it, or anything else you fancied.

Thomas's watch, when he looked at it at last, showed that he had run over their limit – *running into injury-time,* he thought – and he crossed the room to shake Born by the shoulder.

'Come on now, get up, you've had quite enough of that.'

Born sat up and pulled off the plastic shells. There were dark rings under his eyes, and his eyes were watering. He rubbed his face hard with the heels of both hands, grinding them into the eye-sockets like someone woken roughly after sleeping around the clock.

'That was the oddest thing,' he said. 'I think I must have dropped off to sleep. Sorry.'

'You weren't asleep.'

'How could you tell?'

'You've done it before, you know.'

'And what's the difference?'

'You have a tendency to snore.'

Born got up and opened a window, leaning out over the court and filling his lungs.

'Thanks a lot,' he said, with his back to Thomas. He came back into the room. 'Perhaps you can explain this, then.'

'I'll have a try.'

'First of all, let's get this straight. I haven't seen the book.'

'So you say.'

'It was given to me sealed, and you opened it. After yesterday's session, you took it away. It's an Italian publication, and won't be in any of the libraries.'

'I could check that, if necessary. That wouldn't have stopped you discussing it with Wiston.'

'Believe me, I haven't.' Born rubbed his eyes again. 'Now listen to me carefully. What you were looking at was a picture of a mirror. It was round and hard and black, about nine inches across and half an inch thick, with a handle of the same material, all in one piece, with a hole in it. It could have been round or oval; I got the impression that someone was turning it around in their hands, looking at it from all angles.'

Thomas nodded. Born was staring at him hard.

'I saw my face in it.'

'You what?'

'My face, I saw my face in the mirror, reflected in it, and when you moved it round . . . the face seemed to go too, the other way.'

'That's simple optics,' said Thomas, finding comfort in the concept of an ordered universe.

'Now this next bit really was a daydream, or a nightmare, but you'll have to bear with me –'

'If it happened under the Ganzfeld we shall have to record it. Nothing's non-trivial.'

'However trivial it seems?'

'It's a scientific term.'

'And a scientific method?'

'As I understand it, yes.'

'And you'll write it all up later on? Publish a paper, perhaps?'

'If there's anything to go on, anything repeatable, I don't see why not.'

'I'm afraid you'll find this all rather fanciful and odd.'

'Stop beating about the bloody bush, will you, and get on with it. At this stage there'll be good psychological reasons for whatever you have to say, no matter how daft it sounds.' Thomas ruled a line across the open page of his notebook and chewed the end of his pencil. Born lit a cigarette.

'I'm going to call this a vision. You mustn't interrupt me once I start telling you about it, or I shall lose the thread.'

Thomas snorted, and started to write.

'Now.' Born stopped, swallowed and started again. 'We have a street somewhere, with steps going down, and people in tall hats. The steps come up from the river, and there are boats on the river, and people in the boats.'

'Where is all this?'

'In Eastern Europe somewhere, I could tell by the roofs, but I don't know exactly where or when.'

'Don't be daft, where did you see this? What's it got to do with mirrors?'

'So it is a mirror, in the picture?'

'Course it's a bloody mirror. It's in the –'

'No, don't tell me. I'd rather not know. I was hoping . . . it didn't exist.'

'So first you saw your face in it, and then . . .'

'After I'd looked at my face for a while, the mirror got clearer, and then it turned away at an angle, as if something had jerked it round, and I got this astonishing sight for an absolute fraction of a second of a face staring up at me from the side. Someone much shorter than me, with a great shock of straight black hair and a . . . a wide face.'

'How wide?'

Born gestured with his hands.

'Too wide. Perhaps it was distorted, like the mirror, out of perspective.'

'Would you know it if you saw it again?'

'Would I bloody know it.'

Thomas scribbled in his notebook.

'So this . . . face was in the street beside you, was it?'

'No, let me remember: I saw my face, the mirror turned, I saw this other face and . . . when the mirror turned back I was looking out over the river, with the steps leading down.'

'Now, let's try and sort this out. You were looking into the mirror, full on, then it turned at an angle, and when it turned back, you could see your face again, and the street . . .'

'No, when the mirror turned back it was more like a lens, or a convex stone, with the vision happening inside it.'

'Inside it?'

'About an inch into the surface of the stone. Not as if it was going on behind my back, which is what it would have looked like otherwise. The steps led down – all this was happening in the stone –'

'Yes, it's a stone mirror.'

'Stone or black glass, very hard and cold to the touch. I was standing behind a group of people in tall hats and fur coats and cloaks, following them down the steps. They were getting into a rowing-boat, a kind of ferry, and going across the river. The boatmen were standing at their oars, and were shouting and waving at each other, and the people in the boats were joining in. I got in after them, though this was all happening inside the stone and I was outside it, but if I looked down I could see the bottom-boards of the boat and the feet of the other men in long, square-toed shoes with buckles, and we crossed over to the other side. I could see the whole town on the side of a hill, lots of steeples and spires and towers and turrets, very castellated and spiky.'

'But not here?'

'Good God, no. Miles away. You see, we'd crossed the channel, horrible rough crossing, and we nearly got cast up on a sandbank somewhere, and my wife . . . yes, my wife was with me, she must have been with me then, though later . . . and his wife was worried about the winds, gusting quite strongly, but he held on to her . . . you'll just have to let me ramble on. I'll get back to the point in a minute. When we had crossed the river, they took us to a great house beside the wharf, like a cross between a palace and a warehouse, and led us up to the top of the building where there was a room with no windows, but a fire in the middle, no chimney either, a room full of people watching, and they made me, they made me, oh Christ, oh Christ, no, no, it's all right, no, oh Christ, damn it, it's gone again. No, that's it. Finished. No more. I can't remember the rest. That's all there was. I woke up then.' He got up and walked about the room, swinging his arms. 'God, what a load of codswallop, don't you think, ultimately?'

Thomas kept his head down, and filled the page with his neat writing. He thought, *it is a physical process, a concentration too great . . . he threw himself into it, in a painful way, and his energy . . .*

'No, I don't think so. Even if you made it up, I don't. It's useful. Could be very significant.'

'In what way?'

'You could draw me some pictures, perhaps. Draw me a map, and a plan of the room, some sketches. Write up a full report. You didn't notice what a state it got you into, did you? Quite disturbing to watch. You don't mind if we carry on with this tomorrow?'

'Why should I mind? Now, if you like.'

'You need a break.'

'I'm ready now.'

He lay down again, and prepared himself, covering his eyes and ears.

'Seconds out of the ring,' he said. 'Ready for round two.'

Thomas took the catalogue, and opened it quite deliberately at a picture of an alchemist's room, with a crocodile hanging from the ceiling.

'No, not the crocodile,' said Born from the couch. 'I've seen the crocodile already. I want another look at the mirror, if you don't mind.'

'I don't mind at all,' said Thomas, and turned two pages.

# Chapter

# 11

How many ways may inspiration be sought? Through drunkenness; through solitude; through ecstatic dancing; wrapped in a bullock's hide behind a waterfall like the Gaelic sages; benighted in a wilderness of burning bushes; or here, as now, by staring at a mirror in the mind. If Born's imagination existed, and was not merely a soup of chopped and mingled readings and overhearings, it was a thing out of his control; and when he stopped to consider what he had seen, he was very frightened.

Wiston looked at the green notebook entry for that night, at Thomas's papers, and at Born's letter to his mother which he seems to have written that evening, and which is remarkable only because it says so little. He put the documents into some sort of order, and added a few notes of his own.

The first was the letter.

'Gwyn Thomas and I have been carrying on with the couch-sessions I was telling you about, which get more and more like those cartoons of the psychoanalyst in his office every time we repeat them. I am afraid Thomas is having rather a tedious time of it, as all he has to do is to sit and stare at a page for hours on end, taking the occasional note, while I lie there comfortably in the sort of daydream you get in the morning when the alarm has just gone off, and you decide to take another ten minutes in bed before facing the day.

'In these experiments, everything you notice has to be recorded: I write my notes meticulously, like a diary, after telling Thomas the gist of what I have seen. He then goes away and compares the two versions, and comes back the next day looking very sagacious, saying nothing, no doubt having come to the most devastating scientific conclusions about my habits and personality. What a give-away! I'm not sure he's the person I'd trust with the innermost secrets of my psyche, but it's all for the good of the cause, whatever that may be, and holding things back for whatever reason, no matter how tempting, won't answer any questions.'

*I must remark on Born's style in these letters home: it does not change throughout the period leading up to his death, and seems less to reflect his own personality than his interpretation of his mother's. A psychologist might sniff at this judgment, but after meeting her once or twice at the nursing-home and again, briefly, at the funeral, I must say that this impression was strongly reinforced. Odd that she should not have been more perturbed by the content of the letters . . . but perhaps she barely read them.* The letter continues.

'It seems that Wiston is planning to have Thomas to supper tomorrow evening, tête-à-tête in his rooms. I hope to get an amusing report from one or the other. If I do, I'll pass it on. I'm not sure how well Thomas's idea of a jolly evening, revolving as it does around a television supper with the wife and kids, will map on to Wiston's more baroque mode of entertainment. What will happen if he makes Thomas sing for his supper? Verses from Bread of Heaven and a run-through of some hymns and arias, most probably. If I know Wiston, though, he'll try and get him really drunk. And if I know Thomas, that will take some doing. If any further Fellowships crop up, or I get elected to the Society for Psychical Research, I'll write and let you know. And if you hear anything go bump in the night, it will either be Thomas tuning in on your brainwaves, or Wiston on his broomstick, flying round the chimneypots. Love, John.'

*Thomas's notes for the same evening are more clinical, but contain certain matters of interest, so I will add them.*

'2030: Discussion with B. how next part of expt. is to go. Decide on timed random exposures over 10 min. period, 60 sec. each, using cat.

'1040–1050: Ten random pictures from cat: l.h. page only.

| | | |
|---|---|---|
| 1 | p.34 | print, figs. in landscape taking measurements with surveyor's instruments. |
| 2 | p.18 | photo, astrolabe. |
| 3 | p.44 | photo, mirror, as prev. expt. |
| 4 | p. 6 | photo, apothecary's jars. |
| 5 | p.44 | as above. |
| 6 | p.36 | print, bot. illust. (mandrake). |
| 7 | p.22 | print. zodiac. |
| 8 | p.44 | as above, mirror. |
| 9 | p. 6 | as above. |
| 10 | p.44 | as above. |

N.B. catalogue getting creased, spine showing signs of wear, making book fall open at same page.
Analysis: Nos. 2, 3, 5, 8, 9, 10 came through clearly, to some extent. Continues to report odd shadows in mirror (3, 5, 8, 10). Observe that he is picking up my mental

orientation of mirror, e.g. turning through 3 dimen. Has impression that figures are moving. Remains outwardly calm, unsurprised.
Drawings, sketches: These remain confined, as far as representations of objects are concerned, to shaded line drawings. As for representations of the 'visions' in the 'mirror', showing houses, river, boats etc.: his general impression is Germanic or Slavic, at some historical period, probably Czech or Polish. *Not* nightmarish, but disturbing, esp. the *face*, which reappears, typically at start of vision, as before.
N.B. These images do not correspond in any way to my own mental processes during the sessions, and bear no relation to anything I remember having seen or read, Born ditto.

'2nd session: 30 min. 2100–2130. See Born's notes.' *These follow*:

'First five minutes: strong sense of time and place, no sense of Ganzfeld dimension. Discomfort in small of back. (*This disjointed syntax is tiresome to the eye*, noted Wiston, *so I have taken the editorial liberty of amplifying these Sybilline utterances into proper sentences*. The rest follows in Wiston's handwriting, and the original pages are missing.)

'In this session Thomas used only the page with the mirror. The circular form came into focus after ten or fifteen minutes, coming closer and closer. Forms began to appear in the surface, and I was terrified of seeing the *face* again. A large proportion of the figures in the previous vision had their backs to me, and I felt I was following them in procession to some destination or other. This time, the borders of the mirror enclosed my entire field of vision, and when it tilted, my head moved too. Thomas had promised to keep his head still, and his eyes fixed on the middle of the page. I do not know whether the occasional flickerings of the image were due to his blinking or to his attention wandering, but there were no major interruptions.

'Again, the sense of a continuous narrative was a strong one, and repeated the previous vision. The cloaked party in boats came again to the room in the palace by the wharf, but this time the room was a lofty one, large and ornate, with a table in the centre where the fire had been. I stood beside the table, and the group gathered round me. It was a dreamlike state, as before, and I did not have a strong sense of my position in the room. I could still see my own face in the mirror: it gave the impression that I was looking through my own reflection, that I was an immaterial observer looking into a scene at which I was present myself.

'They had set an object on the table, something black and rough, and that increased the feeling of darkening and concentration. I cannot explain this. There was some relation between the object and myself. After a while it filled the mirror, and I felt a strong sense of obligation towards it, of duty, as if it were something I should worship or obey. Again, I cannot explain this feeling. The object was lit by a bright light, brighter than the candles and the torches in the room, and the light grew stronger and stronger until the object itself began to change colour and to shine. I could see reflections in its surface, like those you get in the surface of a brass instrument, not inverted but the right way round, so that your right hand becomes the reflection's right, not his left as usually occurs. I had, too, the disturbing impression of someone standing at my back, but I had no wish to turn round, or ability to do so.'

Wiston noted that the style and content of this report bore a strong similarity to those of other séances: one expected tambourines and trumpets. The strange thing was, in all these notes, that there was no pretence of anything occurring outside Born's mind: he was reporting only his hallucinations, without pretending they had any external existence, and without attempting to apply any sort of objective, logical analysis. Finally, there was another letter in Born's hand, again addressed to his mother.

'I'm afraid you'll think I'm wasting my time with these sessions, when I could be writing up my work: but I must say again that we seldom start until after dinner and, as I've told you before, I've been putting in a regular nine-to-seven day in the library. My interest in the subject is mainly due to the fact that this is one area where science and the arts come close together: we are dealing in matters of the imagination, where there is no control over what is being produced, beyond the rather debatable influence of Thomas and the pictures in the book.

'The Ganzfeld provides the force, or rather the isolation in which the force of the imagination – the fancy, to use the older term – can operate. And do not suppose that I am trying to spin him a yarn: I am telling him exactly what I see. If it is my imagination and its workings that interest him, that should satisfy his curiosity.

'There are no drugs involved, either: we're not on LSD or mescalin or the other psychotropic or hallucinogenic drugs: nothing stronger than coffee before and a pint in the college bar at the end of the session – and by God I'm needing it by then. It is a strange experience, but the strangeness stops – now, at least – as soon as the eyepieces and the headphones are off and I can see and hear again. Thomas tells me we hardly use our brains to anything like their full capacity: that in itself is a challenge. I'm just waiting for the voices to start.'

# Chapter 12

Wiston planned his dinner for Thomas with care. Thomas rarely dined in hall as he found the atmosphere intimidating, and he preferred to eat with his wife at home, so Wiston decided to provide a special treat in his own rooms. The college staff, invaluable on such occasions, rose happily to his requests, approved his choice of dishes, and even arranged for Mr Slim the butler to wait at table. Wiston managed to borrow from the Manciple some of the finer pieces of college silver, and laid the dinner-table elegantly with Caroline cutlery, silver beakers chased with hunting-scenes, a pair of Georgian candlesticks and an elaborate Victorian table-decoration, a gift to the college from an officers' mess, depicting camels, palm-trees and a Bedouin tent. The table was covered with fine damask linen, and cream-coloured roses filled a great silver bowl on the sideboard. All was white, shining, purificatory. Mr Slim in a tail-coat stood at his post, and Wiston went to dress for dinner, remembering only at the last minute, when it was too late, that he had forgotten to mention that they would be dining formally, if intimately, and that dress was to be black tie.

The time on the invitation was seven-thirty for eight. At seven twenty-five by the clock in the courtyard, Thomas arrived, out of breath, clutching his card in his hand as if he expected it to be torn in half at the door. Mr Slim kept him waiting until Wiston had tied his tie, and let him in only after the clock had struck, melodiously, the half hour.

Thomas was wearing in honour of the occasion a grey suit quite decently pressed, with a red thread somewhere in the weave, and a clothing-mart approximation to a regimental tie. Wiston, bearing in mind his *faux pas* with the invitation, over which he had taken infinite pains with an italic nib and sepia ink, refrained from his usual internal commentary on Thomas's costume and manners, and welcomed him with greater enthusiasm than might have been called for.

'My dear Thomas, how terribly nice of you to come. I wasn't sure whether to expect you, as I imagined that your wife and family had a greater call . . . so sorry I couldn't ask them too.'

'I put a note in the lodge in the middle of yesterday afternoon. I could have slipped it under your door, if I'd thought.'

Mr Slim, with an automatic motion, produced a decanter of mahogany-coloured sherry and two glasses.

'Sweet or dry?'

'Dry for me, if it's all the same.'

'Oh my God, I don't think I put it to chill . . . If you can stand it at room temperature . . .' Wiston waved his hands helplessly in the air, and Mr Slim, following his instructions to the letter, went to the kitchen and returned with another decanter that had been standing close to the stove. He poured a glass of it for Thomas, and one from the first decanter for Wiston, who was glad to see Thomas's eyes begin to bulge as the dark liquid trickled into the glass.

'I have a sweet tooth, as you can see.' Wiston drained his glass, and held it out for Mr Slim to refill. The butler was even taller than Wiston, and beetled over Thomas, who found himself at a loss for an answer, and knocked back his sherry instead. His glass was no sooner emptied than filled again: 'Make sure he gets enough to drink,' Wiston had instructed Mr Slim, 'and see that he feels at home. He isn't used to company, so put him at his ease.'

'*Iach y da!*' toasted Wiston, raising his glass to the light.

'*Iach y da*.' Thomas replied, without enthusiasm.

Wiston watched him gazing at the silver and congratulated himself on his choice of pieces: the centrepiece particularly seemed to catch his eye, and Wiston leant forward to demonstrate how the jointed silver palm-trees would sway when touched, and how the Bedouin could be taken out of their tent and made to sit on the sand.

'Very ingenious,' said Thomas, trying the mechanism himself. 'But why go to all this trouble for the two of us?'

'Oh, sometimes I feel I owe myself a treat,' said Wiston, holding out his glass again. 'And what could be more pleasant than to be waited on in your own rooms, with good wine, good food, moderate company, and no duties left undone.'

'Talking of duties, how is your own work going?' asked Thomas. It was a subject he always enjoyed, though one that by convention could never be discussed at High Table.

'Oh, don't let us talk about work,' said Wiston. 'There are far more interesting things we have to do. Now do sit down, I believe we are almost ready to eat.' He rang a silver bell, and Mr Slim appeared in the doorway with a covered dish of artichokes and a jug of mayonnaise.

'You'll have to show me how to deal with these,' said Thomas. A *meat-and-potatoes man* thought Wiston, *and no fancy business*. He nodded to Mr Slim, who leant across his shoulder, peeled off an outside leaf, dipped it in mayonnaise and drew it between his teeth. Thomas tried the same experiment, finding to his dismay that the mayonnaise seemed to have been compounded of pure garlic, which burned his mouth like mustard. Mr Slim filled his glass with Moselle, and he drank it rapidly to quench his thirst.

'I should have warned you about the mayonnaise,' said Wiston. 'It's a rather powerful Roman recipe: you take half a pint of the best olive oil and twelve cloves of garlic, pound them in a mortar –'

'All right, I get the picture,' said Thomas, and ate the rest of his artichoke ungarnished.

'Such a silly food,' said Wiston, when he had finished. 'More left on the plate than you had when you started. And pretty indigestible, too. I wonder people bother with it, but I love the flavour.'

'It's a wonder to me you can taste it, under all that garlic,' said Thomas, wishing for a toothpick.

'I thought the Welsh had a fondness for the family of alliums,' said Wiston. 'I hope you have: there's leek soup to follow. *And whoever ate leeks that weren't full of grit?* he thought; *not Thomas, not this time*.

Carp followed the soup, on a bed of rice, and Wiston made a pantomime of lifting the flesh away from the bones, and burrowing for the kernel of meat below the eye. Even so, he noticed that Thomas was having difficulty with the tiny spines, and that each mouthful went down painfully, with much swallowing and many sips of wine.

'I've a theory that the best things about the colleges go

back to monastic times,' said Wiston, conversationally, 'and the great thing about the monasteries was their self-sufficiency. I have long been trying to persuade the Bursar to let us have a carp-pond in the garden, not those vulgar goldfish but the great old carp that come to you when you clap your hands, and take bread from your fingers. Live for two hundred years, I believe. This one came out of the river, which accounts for the muddy flavour. I understand one should let them swim around in a bowl of milk for a day or two before eating them, but the college kitchens will pay no such attention to detail. Lampreys are another thing I've always wanted to try, but so far they have eluded me. Do have some more wine.'

Thomas, happy to have been excused lampreys, emptied his glass and held it out for Mr Slim to fill.

'You often find some nice wines to go with a somewhat unusual fish,' said Wiston, thinking *but this isn't one of them*. He sipped at a glass of water. *It should dissolve the fishbones, though.* He rang for the next course.

'Since we are past the Glorious Twelfth . . .' Wiston announced, lifting the silver cover off the dish, 'I thought a grouse might be in order. I hope they've made sure it was properly hung, though. Nothing worse than under-hung game.' *Nothing, that is, except over-hung game, and by Jove . . .*

'Don't crack a filling on a stray bit of shot,' he said, as Thomas bit into a slice of breast-meat and pulled a face. 'Slim, you're sure it was hung long enough?'

'Couldn't have stood another day, sir,' said Mr Slim. 'Not in this close hot weather.'

Thomas looked doubtful, and had long since given up the struggle to converse, but stuck to his glass.

'At least the burgundy is good,' said Wiston, 'And there's more where it came from, so drink up.'

After the grouse came mutton, and the mutton was followed by burnt creams, then dried figs, nuts and coffee for dessert. The cream had been cooked in little bowls, after the college's fashion, and the sugar coating browned under a salamander, setting when cool to a glassy hardness. Thomas cracked at his with a spoon and broke the bowl, splashing his suit with custard: Mr Slim came forward with a cloth and mopped at him until he felt more foolish than before, while Wiston smiled, nodded and ate his pudding.

The coffee, instant in a Queen Anne pot, finished the meal, and Wiston insisted that Thomas should join him in a glass of a greenish-black Italian *digestivo*, a bitter draught of astringent herbs designed to wring the tastebuds and jerk the sluggish liver into action. Thomas drained his glass with the expression of a man climbing the last fence on an assault-course, and followed Wiston out of the dining-room with his bladder bursting and his head beginning to spin.

Wiston led him into his parlour, a cold, uncomfortable room where he taught his pupils. The walls were dark Pompeian red, and hard chairs stood all around them. There were no pictures, and the central light had a flimsy parchment shade that cast harsh shadows into the corners and swung in any draught. It was like a waiting-room at a country station, and the fireplace was the familiar ugly cast-iron affair, black-leaded and empty of coals. Mr Slim had put a little round one-legged table on the rug in the centre of the room, under the light, and Wiston, before sending him home, drew up two chairs from beside the fire, leaving an unsymmetrical gap. The red walls, hard chairs and harsh overhead light made it a comfortless place to sit after dinner, but Wiston did not want to linger over the broken meats and the silver in the dining-room, and the music-room was locked. A bottle of grappa and two glasses stood on the table, and Wiston sat down. Thomas made an excuse and left the room at a trot, and Wiston heard him fumbling at the handles of various doors on his way to the lavatory, and hoped, if he felt sick, he would not leave a mess to clear up. He waited for the unreliable cistern to flush, and poured spirit into the glasses.

'Those lemon geraniums smell a treat,' said Thomas, rubbing his hands dry and preparing to enjoy the rest of the evening. 'I still can't get rid of the taste of that green liquor, though. I thought you were playing a joke.' *One of a number,* thought Wiston, and gave him a glass of grappa.

'A good *digestivo* is the best thing in the world to finish off a meal: sets you up for the rest of the evening. Follow it with this, and all your troubles are over.' Grappa is fiery stuff, and Wiston had kept a bottle for drinking on certain occasions, when there was nothing else to hand. In the cold red room – the day's heat had almost gone, and was pointing to the approach of the fall – the spirit warmed them both. Wiston filled their glasses again, and Thomas decided to write off the following morning's work as an unviable concept. He was well on his way, Wiston was pleased to observe, to being thoroughly drunk. Thomas anchored his feet on the rug, his heels sliding on the polished boards, and started to talk.

'We're been working on the project, now, for quite a few days. I expect Born's mentioned it to you.'

Wiston nodded, and smiled encouragingly.

'No particularly earth-shattering discoveries as yet, mind you, but we've come upon some unexpected results, the sort of thing that could make quite a splash. I definitely get the impression that we're on to something big.'

His face was red and his throat was straining at the

collar: Wiston wanted to lean forward and loosen it for him, undoing the button and tugging at the knot of the tie, to make him relax and feel more comfortable.

'Of course, it's outside my normal line of country, which is why I'm not too keen on news of it getting back to the department before I'm ready to start writing up the results. But it's beginning to hang together, and a lot of the details mesh in with my previous work, corroborate some of my data, you know, and there's plenty to fit in with my previous theories, but I must say the most exciting thing about it –'

'Yes?' Wiston leaned forward in his chair.

'Well, it's early days yet, but from what I can make of the evidence . . .' Thomas shuffled his feet on the rug under the table, reminding Wiston of a nervous pupil facing his tutor on a Monday morning with his work unprepared. 'It seems we're getting something along the lines of a historical perspective. A sort of spiritual *déjà vu*.'

'Oh? In what way?'

'It's just that . . . it reminded me, what he was saying, and of course I can't go into details, of something I read in a magazine. In the waiting-room at the surgery, as a matter of fact. Apparently, what it said was, there are states of mind when people start getting, you know, flashes from the past, scenes from their former lives . . . It sounds daft, I know, and I bet you weren't expecting to hear anything like this from a scientist, even when he's drunk, but there you are.'

Wiston tilted his chair on its back legs, and let out a hiss of air.

'This sounds breathtaking. It sounds as if you're on the edge of a real breakthrough. Do you mean to say that you and Born are getting, under experimental conditions, in a laboratory, the sort of results that mediums have been striving after for years?'

'Well, it's hardly a laboratory, and as for experimental conditions . . . But yes, that would be one way of putting it. Yes.'

The wine and the red-walled room were making Wiston's own head feel light, as if the conversation had been taking place between disembodied voices in an empty room. Thomas was slipping slowly to one side on his narrow chair.

'I hope you'll be writing this up fairly shortly. Make sure you get the article published somewhere prominent, a newspaper rather than an academic journal, I'd suggest. It's such a pity that specialist articles in every field are ignored because the wider audience can't get access to the publications. Ultimately, we are both philosophers, more so perhaps than our friend Born; it is the beginning and the end of all our concerns, and a wider general knowledge can only add to the depth of thinking inside each specialization. Of course, I'm interested in the psychology behind your work as well, in the general motivation of the project. There's always more below the surface than appears at first. So don't be surprised if you find more to Born than meets the eye. I wouldn't put it past him to spring a few surprises on you. Tell me, what do you think of him? His work, his prospects, speaking as a colleague? No, don't bother to answer, that was an unfair question to ask. I'm sure you're as concerned about him as I am. It's always alarming when someone's work dries up on him, or when he feels he has been labouring for years in vain and unappreciated: he's apt to clutch at any straw. All's fair, you know, and opposition may be found in unexpected quarters. Watch out he doesn't beat you into print and pip you at the post. But remember, go for one of the popular dailies, don't hide your light under a bushel.'

The only question that formed itself in Thomas's mind was whether he could negotiate the distance from the table to the door, the door to the stairs, and the stairs into the court.

'Could you give me an arm to hang on to,' he said, looking towards Wiston with his eyes unfocused. 'I believe I've taken a glass or two above my limit.'

Wiston took him by the elbow and guided him to the door.

''S all right, I can find my own way home,' said Thomas, tripping over the step down to the door and saving himself on the banister. 'I'd like . . . I'd like to say thanks for the dinner, and your most . . . delightful . . . hospitality.' Wiston returned to his room, and heard Thomas taking the stairs gently, overstepping the turn at the landing, rallying at the bottom and coming out with a rush into the court, where he was sick on the steps of the fountain. Wiston took the bottle and the glasses off the table, and turned out all the lights.

# Chapter 13

'Dear Mother, poor Thomas has just had rather an ordeal, courtesy of our common friend Dr Wiston: one of those dreadful dinners where they dish up everything from grouse to artichokes when all you want is a well-done steak and a grilled tomato. He really gave him the works: college silver, Mr Slim the butler (sounds like Happy Families) in black and white from head to foot, Wiston ditto, having "forgotten" to tell Thomas to dress up, officiating at the obsequies of the nastiest, most obstreperous dishes he says he's ever eaten, and finishing up with a draught of what sounds, from its flavour and effect on the system, like a dose of brake-fluid. Thomas turned up here this afternoon, having spent the night where you might imagine, and looking more washed out than I've seen him. What his wife must have said I can easily guess. He was quite convinced that Wiston put on the whole show to make him look small.

'When he gets back from the chemist's (aspirin's the only cure, and that's only effective after three o'clock) we shall carry on with the next couch-session, and see how far we can take things. I have the feeling that we are about to enter a new phase, and I have decided to do some more research towards it on my own, in the hope of making an original contribution. I am keeping a detailed diary, as well as giving my notes to Thomas at the end of each session, and we discuss the results. He's writing it up as well, but I think there will be a few alterations to be made to his own notes, as I am not being entirely straightforward with him. I'm afraid if I were, he'd have me certified. Only joking.

'The difference between the two accounts – the first written immediately after "waking up" from the Ganzfeld state, and the second the following day – is quite significant in itself, as perception of hallucinatory states in retrospect can be quite different from the first account, almost as if the visions had been developing slowly after the event, like photographic images.

'What I plan to do, though, is rather different. You know I have a cassette recorder I never use? Well, I am thinking of taping a dictated diary, a private one, in case there are any points I want to keep out of the main record. This isn't being unscientific or devious: I just have the feeling that it will be more useful to Thomas if I present it to him at a later date, when he's ready to write up his final paper. It's bound to come out in some prestigious journal, and will either make or break his reputation: you can imagine how risky it is for a scientist in an established field to go out on a limb with something as controversial as this.

'Even so, I must say he was very cagey when I asked him what he planned to do with the report when it's finished, almost as if he thought I was going to step in and jump the gun. I haven't been offered a co-authorship, but after all, it is Thomas's baby, and I don't think I could summon up the jargon. Guinea-pigs aren't expected to write their own experiment-reports, so I shall just lie back and enjoy it, and let him take the credit.

'It actually is quite enjoyable, and I rather like being studied, if only by Thomas, who can be a bit dull at times. Wiston is showing a gratifying amount of interest in the project, too, which is encouraging. The idea of having one's every word, thought and daydream taken down and analysed for its psychical content pleases my self-conceit no end, and gives me a great temptation to romanticize, which I hope I shall resist. There's enormous scope for composing elaborate fictions, and spinning him a good long yarn. What a way of getting a story into print: in the pages of a scientific journal!

'But I shan't be spending the whole vacation flat on my back (much as I'd like to) as there is a lot of work that has suddenly cropped up for me to do in London: I can foresee long afternoons in the British Library deciphering parchments in the Manuscripts Room, all in different coloured inks, with charts that fold out and show magical insignia: if you mutter them under your breath, the librarians turn into frogs and the Reading Room dome shuts up like an umbrella. But I can hear Thomas's heavy foot upon the stair, so I shall sign off and run for the post.'

Wiston wondered, as he studied this letter, how Born's mother had failed to see the danger-signals: Born's fear of madness, his visions, his temptations into fantasy, his uncharacteristic interest in occult documents in the British Library . . . *But perhaps*, he thought, *she never read the letter: just opened it, glanced at it and put it on one side.*

Thomas came in, looking no better, and sat on the couch, propping his forehead on his palms.

'Feeling any livelier?'

'Not a lot.'

'Come and sit down. Have a cup of coffee. Black and medicinal. That'll do the trick. Or some nice weak China tea.'

'I'm not letting anything near that part of my anatomy for another week and a half.'

'Grousing at another man's hospitality . . .'

'I'll give you bloody grouse. I've still got the taste at the back of my mouth. And the garlic! Ach!'

Thomas groaned, and held his head again.

'What are we going to do, then? Admit he's sabotaged the session yet again?'

'No, no, we'll carry on with it. You've got something to read to me, if I remember.'

'Yes, I've written up the diary. I noticed quite a few differences between the two accounts. I expect you'll want to go over them when you make your report.'

'I recall hearing some remark from Wiston on the subject last night, but I was too tired to listen properly.'

'Tired and emotional?'

'That besides. No, I can't say I remember now. Struck me as significant at the time. You could see about some tea, if you like.'

Born fetched tea and gave a cup to Thomas, who nursed it in his lap as if it were the only source of heat in a frigid universe.

'All I need to read out is the bit where the two mirrors started to come together.'

'Two mirrors?'

'Well, there was the first one, the black one, the one that starts the visions off, and then there has been a second one showing up from time to time. You know I said I'd started to get the impression of a fairly concerted narrative?'

'Yes?'

'Well, this seems to be the mechanism it works by, a

sort of step-by-step progression.'

'You'd better read it out.' Thomas took a tentative sip at his tea.

'This takes the story up from the moment of being shown the black object on the table, the one that changed colour. *I tried to reach out and hold it, and it seemed to have a handle like the mirror, and when I came closer to it, and let it fill my field of vision, it was the mirror – and you must remember that the vision was taking place in the mirror all the time, rather like a reflection in a reflection. With the feeling of someone standing at my back, it was hard to shake off the idea that they were holding a mirror behind my head, and that that was causing the reflection.* I don't know if that makes things any clearer.'

'None of this seems to be getting us anywhere,' said Thomas, finishing his tea and bracing himself for more. 'It all sounds highly inconsequential.'

'If you'd rather I didn't carry on . . .'

'I'm not sure I can concentrate on it just at the moment. Too much of last night's liquor still sloshing around in my head.'

'I know. I've been fit for nothing today but writing letters home.'

Thomas looked suspiciously at the desk: all that was there, apart from a box of blank paper and a jar of pencils, was the letter to his mother, four sheets folded in three. Thomas craned his head to look at it; Born caught his gesture, took the letter and handed it towards him.

'There, you can read it if you like. Nothing about anything to do with this.' Thomas did not take the letter.

'Wiston knew plenty.'

'How much did he know?'

'Quite a lot, it seemed to me. How much have you been telling him?'

'Hardly a word. Are you sure it wasn't guesswork? He

can read the journals, and it's all in there.'

'It would have to be pretty inspired guesswork.'

'If you're afraid of anyone getting there first . . .'

'I'm not afraid. I just need to be able to trust the people I work with, that's all. And if a fancy dinner-party with some clever-clever antiquarian is enough to make you spill the beans . . . Oh, God, I don't know.' Thomas lowered his head to the arm of his chair, slopping some tea.

'Go home,' said Born deliberately. 'Go home and take a nap for an hour or two, and don't come back till you're feeling better. Sleep it out of your system, and then we'll carry on.'

'Maybe you're right,' said Thomas. 'God, but that was a painful experience. Deserves a week's fasting on bread and water, that does.'

'Go away and do penance,' said Born. 'Three times round the court on the cobbles, on your hands and knees. Then a dip in the fountain, and go home when you're feeling good and shriven.'

Thomas grinned and went down the stairs.

As soon as he had gone, Born took a tape-recorder from his desk, slotted in a blank cassette, and pressed the recording button.

# Chapter 14

This is the text of the tape, in Wiston's annotated transcription.

'I was called to the stone, and the spirit spoke to me out of the stone, and it was a good spirit. I am Uriel, it said, and those around me cried aloud, saying, does he speak to you? And I said, he has told me his name, and his name is Uriel. And he who was standing beside me with the book said, he is the great angel, and I would enquire of him. And I said, what would you ask? And the spirit spoke to me out of the stone, saying, I know his question. And I was afraid, and retired from the stone, into the arms of those around me in the room. And they said, do not be afraid, but go to the stone and speak to the spirit within the stone. And the spirit spoke to me out of my own mouth, saying:

*Gariel zed masch, ich na gel galaat*
*Gemp gal noch Cabalandam . . .'*

*(These words repeated five or six times in an utterly different voice, and with what sounds like a strong Bohemian accent.)*

'Then he called me back to the stone, and showed me his face in the depths of the stone, about as far within the stone as my arm could reach; and I stretched out my arm to touch his face, and it was very bright. And my arm was held from behind and kept from entering the stone. And his face was very bright but cold, and I could see his lips moving in the depths of the stone, but his eyes were still. And the face of the stone was black, but his was very bright.'

*(A curious feature of this part of the vision, apart from its being the first with an auditory element, is that although it bears some relation to the document Born had studied in the British Library, the connection is not entirely clear: for instance, Kelly's narration to Dee includes little or no reference to other people in the room, or to their reaction to his speaking in tongues. I can make little sense of the visionary voice, despite its Slavic or Germanic elements, and assume it to be some form of glossolalia. There is a break in the recording at this point, and the following sounds may be heard in the background: a scraping, as of a chair being pushed back, the word 'Coffee' in Born's voice, and a double click as the apparatus is switched off and on again. Then Born's voice resumes.)*

'Again I tried to take the stone in my hands, but I was prevented as before. I did not turn, nor could I see who was within the stone. The stone is heavy now, too heavy for the table, and the tablets have lost their markings. I must bear up the stone, for it has the world within it. The world is in the stone, not on the face of the stone, but in its depths, and they will show it to me, but not yet. (*Born sips his coffee, the machine still running, with the comment,* "Too black, this coffee, far too black. Enough to give you nightmares. Put some milk in it, then, put some milk in it, take the black away," *then scrapes his chair again, leaves the room, the door banging, returns, curses, then turns the machine off and on again. The voice begins at once.*)

'That's better, much better. Great improvement. Better run over that stuff again, go through it, see what's . . .' (*Machine stopped and started: Born evidently ran over the tape, and clipped some words off the last sentence. This is part of the unreliability of a tape as documentary evidence, the more frustrating in a private case such as this, where there could be no possible motive for concealment. Obviously the more blatant forms of tampering – cutting and splicing, etc. – were beyond Born's technical resources, but apart from a couple of significant gaps in one passage, which may be deliberate omissions or simply pauses, there are few places where one feels that any great amount of testimony is missing.*)

'Pretty startling, that. Pretty unexpected. No, I don't think I shall be playing that through to Thomas, not yet, not just yet. But that's what happened. That is . . . definitely what happened. Twice, three times. Bloody funny about the coffee, though, how . . .' (*A laugh, and the tape is cut again.*) Better go over some of that. Perhaps if I try . . . pencil and paper. Right.' (*Drawer opens and shuts, quite a loud bang, coming up through the desk-top into the machine.*) 'Right. Now . . . the mirror, shade it in, concentrate then . . . over the top . . . face, eyes covered. Why were my eyes uncovered, then, in the stone? If I was wearing . . . no, don't be stupid, all going on underneath them, inside . . . Right, that's okay then, that's sorted out. Better now. Easier to follow, if they transcribe . . . but he's taking it all down, in the book, and I shall have the book.' (*Here his voice changes.*) 'Uriel, yes, Uriel is his name. I heard him speak it. And Gabriel and Raphael and Michael beside him, behind him in the stone. I cannot see their faces or their hands, for they are covered by their wings.

'Now he says to me, question them, in the Lord's name (*erasure*) and there are clouds in the stone, and a sword appears from the cloud, with its tip broken off.

And he writes this down. And he tells me, ask them again, and this time the clouds clear away, and I see two birds, deep within the stone, and the sky is behind them, and there is light on their wings. Then they take a star from one of the constellations, and play with it like a ball, and then . . . it becomes a man's head, with a . . . a broad face and flattened features, like the face . . . the face . . . and the nose is flattened and the cheeks are very full, with the lobes of the ears drawn down to the shoulders. And the corners of the mouth are turned down. Now the birds fly low over the roofs of the city, and cry out, and the walls of the city are broken down. And the head lies on a little hill, and it is both a head and a ball, a children's coloured ball of twelve leather patches sewn together. And the ball and the head are one. And the ball becomes the terrestrial globe, with markings for the land and sea, and clouds passing over the face of the globe. I tell him this, and he writes it down. And I ask him, is your question answered? And he says, Yes, it is answered, but the answer will be hard to interpret. The face has gone, and now the clouds are passing, and I cannot see more than a handsbreadth into the stone.'

*(Again, there is a strong resemblance between this vision and one of those in the documents, but certain passages cannot be explained in that way. For instance, the features of the head seem reminiscent of those colossal stone heads found in Mexico, remnants of great Aztec or Olmec statues whose bodies no longer survive, if they were ever completed. The transformation of the head into a ball, and the ball into a globe, has echoes of a passage in the Phaedo, and of the Vision of Julian of Norwich. Other details are curious: the questioner is never identified or seen: is he the note-taker, in which case he could be identified with Thomas, or Dee himself, another Welshman, all of which raises the further question: did Born ever intend to play the tape to Thomas? Or did he wish all these documents to be discovered*

*as a single testament? Did he foresee his own death, in another unrecorded vision? He certainly never mentioned to me the existence of the tape, and it was by the merest coincidence that I found it, when I came to collect the catalogue, and they were together in the drawer of his desk. The questions of Born's intonation in this recording can best be explained by a musical analogy, with which he would have been familiar: the 'tonic' voice – simple comments about the coffee, etc. – is his normal speaking voice, a not particularly incisive tenor, inclined to rise with excitement, but generally well-modulated and a pleasant contrast to Thomas's repetitive sing-song. When he delivers his more bardic utterances on this tape, he goes to the dominant, a fifth higher, uncomfortably high for his range. This tends to level out the modulations in tone, and the delivery becomes monotonous, like a chaplain preaching in a resonant Gothic chapel and accommodating his voice to the reverberations. The voice of the 'spirit' or 'archangel' Uriel could be a different person: it is the subdominant voice of the three, a fifth below the tonic, with a gruffer, hoarser intonation. Not an angelic voice in any sense, unless a fallen one.)*

It was also odd, Wiston noted, that Born did not give more of this information in his written account of the sessions: it would have been consistent with his motives to make the recording corroborate with the diary; but the diary is ineffective in giving any impression of the immediacy and depth of the visions or hallucinations, whether they were purely the product of a calculating invention, imaginative or heightened daydreams, or had some other origin. Perhaps it was simply that the act of writing (which would have interrupted the flow of words) switched off his memory of these details, just as speaking would have interrupted the Ganzfeld itself: both glossolalia and rambling talk are recorded as symptoms of many hallucinatory, prophetic or visionary states, whether in mythology or in the records of the anthropologist. Wiston's notes introduce the final section of the tape, and continue:

*(This part of the tape may also be of interest. It is delivered in a fourth voice, a high-pitched, affected intonation, a foppish, self-conceited voice.)*

'Lord, Sir, I am the only man in England that can tell you what this might be. Why, Sir, 'tis Doctor Dee's mirror, that Sam Butler called the Devil's Looking-Glass, cut from cannel-coal and brought from Mexico, a great rarity indeed. I have it from his Grace's cabinet, my Lord Frederick Campbell, in a leathern case with some verses upon it. Cannel-coal, sir, like jet, only more fine, more apt to take a finish. It has a fine polish, Sir, you will agree, but I don't like to look at it too deeply, as it is the glass that . . . the King's hop-pillow, too, Sir, as I know you are discreet, is a thing I would dearly love to have, 'twould grace this cabinet of mine as it disgraces his bedchamber and his physicians. A trifle of no value save in the assocation, like this Hat, Sir, that was the great Cardinal's, Thomas Wolsey. And this medallion, gilt, made for His Majesty's late recovery. I had this from a gentleman of the bedchamber for a small consideration: he would gladly change places with me, he said, or any other man in the kingdom, since this last relapse. As sad a decay, Sir, as any in these times. And this plate beside it was Kelly's, his soothsayer that died from a fall, and is made of a plate of the transmuted metal, so they say. No, Sir, Dee's soothsayer, la! how you jest! No, if I were to see my face in it, that would be fright enough. But 'tis a pretty thing, among all my pretty things, and a pretty room, with a fair view. Pars drew it from this very window, in a morning, and I stood beside his shoulder as he worked, with the strongest sensation . . . of another at my back, until upon an impulse I turned and covered the looking-glass with a cloth, and returned it to its case.

From Mortlake to Twickenham is no great distance, and if the Doctor will pay a visit, he must ring the bell or come by appointment. If I am to be haunted in my own home, let it be by arrangement. We keep an orderly household, Sir. But the King, too, sees visions and hears voices, visions and voices, so I pray you will keep silence on this matter. Now, Sir, the mirror back to its case, too kind, Sir, remember me to his Grace . . .'

*(N.B. These notes to the above passage were made as soon as I had had the tape transcribed: a great deal has happened since then which has caused me to alter my judgment considerably about these and other matters, but they may stand as a record of my opinions in the week of his death.)*

# Chapter 15

From his study window, Wiston watched Thomas returning across the court towards Born's rooms: his nap had done him good, and he walked with a spring in his step like a man who had done a worthwhile afternoon's business. There was a secretive tilt to his head, that said 'I know something that you don't know' as clearly as if he had sung it aloud. This jauntiness made Wiston think that his researches were going unexpectedly well, and when he asked Thomas not many days later, in the entrance-hall of the private nursing-home where Born was lying, what it was that had made him so cheerful, he said only that an unexpected meeting and a telephone-call had brightened his prospects.

When Thomas came to Born's room he found him sitting at his desk, facing the wall. He did not turn round when Thomas came in, although he had knocked three times. Thomas crossed the room and tapped him on the shoulder, but still Born did not turn, and instead began to tremble slightly, as someone timid of spiders will tremble if a thread brushes his neck.

'Come on, it's only me,' said Thomas soothingly, his voice falling and rising, falling and rising like the contours of a Welsh valley.

'Oh, there you are,' said Born, as if he had been looking for him all over town, and had come upon him suddenly in a distant street. 'There you are.'

'What are you up to? Falling into a trance behind my back?'

'Oh, sitting and staring into space, what does it look like? I can stare for hours at a mark on the wall. Passes the time wonderfully.'

'Why don't arts students stare out of the window in the mornings?' asked Thomas, like a man telling a joke.

'I give up.'

'They'd have nothing to do in the afternoons, then, would they? Go on, you've got to laugh.'

Born gave a high-pitched, artificial giggle, showing his teeth.

'God, you've got it bad, haven't you. I thought I was the one with the funny head,' said Thomas, propping one buttock on the desk-top. 'Bet you don't know what I've been doing all afternoon. Bet you're dying to know.'

Born shook his head slowly from side to side, far too many times. Thomas wanted to steady it between his palms. In the end, the shaking became imperceptible, and Born continued to stare at the wall.

Thomas told Wiston afterwards, 'I thought he was having one of those moods, you know, artistic temperament catching up with him, like throwing a fit of the sulks to get a bit of attention. I should have had more sense than ask him to carry on in that state of mind.' But now all he said was:

'Oh, well, I shan't tell you, then. Look, are we going to have this famous session of ours, or aren't we?'

Born turned suddenly round in his chair, and became

more animated, but his face was still pale and his pupils were dilated, and there were dark rings around his eyes. 'Looked as if he'd seen something nasty in the woodshed, to tell you the honest truth. He'd got that tape-recorder on the desk in front of him, and I didn't think to ask what he was doing with it. I should have, I suppose, but you don't, do you?' Using you for 'I' or one is a good transmitter of blame, and Thomas used it a lot in the last few days, to Wiston and to anyone else who came near him.

'Yes, I think we ought to get on with it right away,' said Born, more cheerfully. 'I want to know what happens next.'

'There's nothing you want to add to what you've read me?'

'You sound like a police enquiry. Is there anything you wish to append to your statement as it stands, any further information you can recollect that may be pertinent to our enquiries? Would you like us to jog your memory a little before you put your signature to the final draft?' Born's comical Inspector Plod delivery put Thomas back at his ease, and they laughed together, Thomas relieved that the high-pitched cackling had stopped.

Born went over to the couch: where the heels of his shoes had touched the cover, there were now faint black marks, and other dents and hollows at shoulder, head and hips showed his dimensions clearly, like the body's imprint on a shroud. The couch had become, in both their minds, a more significant part of the Ganzfeld mechanism than the headphones or the absurd clown-mask of the pop-eyed blinkers: it was the puppet-master's stage, the operating-table.

'How long do you think you can take?'

'As long as you're prepared to sit and watch. I have a

feeling this will only take a short time, and I want to get it over as soon as I can. So the longer the better.'

'I'll give you an hour and a half.'

'Oh, well, in that case . . .' Born left the room.

Thomas waited for the lavatory door to bang shut, and went silently to the desk. The green notebook was lying on the tape-recorder, and he opened the cover and leafed through. Everything in the last few pages was as Born had told him, but they were untidily written and the pages had no headings or subtitles, with nothing to show that Born was planning to write them up.

'Bloody Wiston putting the cat among the pigeons,' he said, and sat down at the desk with the catalogue opened at the familiar page. Its spine was broken now, and the leaf with the picture of the mirror was coming loose. *This is a book,* thought Thomas unrepentantly, *that falls naturally into two parts.* It pleased him to imagine Wiston painfully mending it with library tape: books were for use, and if they were read to pieces, at least it showed they had been used well. *If he's fool enough to lend his books around,* he thought, *that's what he should expect,* and he tugged maliciously at the page, loosening it further. There was a noise of falling water, and Thomas swivelled in his chair so that he could look Born in the face as he came through the door.

People often do not pull their company faces until they are well inside the room, the cheerful smile of greeting and welcome, sincere or insincere, slipping into place a split second too late. Born's face reminded Thomas of a little rhyme, which he began to quote aloud.

*'As I was coming up the stair,'* said Thomas, *'I met a man who wasn't there.'*

Born started to tremble.

*'He wasn't there again today,'* Thomas continued. *'I wish that man would –'*

'Will you shut up, for pity's sake?' Born cried in a loud voice, and went and stood at the window, where Wiston could see him, with his arms outstretched.

'Sorry I spoke, said Thomas, quite baffled. 'Pardon me for living, I'm sure.'

Born gripped the window-sill hard, and pressed his forehead against the pane, so that from across the court it looked as white as bone. Then he let his shoulders come unknotted, went over to the couch and lay on his back, his eyes shut, his hands at his sides.

Thomas attended to the laying-out, sellotaping the halved ping-pong balls over the eyes and packing them round with cotton-wool, adjusting the headphones over the ears, then plugging them into the amplifier, and the amplifier to the white-noise generator. Born reached out and twiddled at the volume control until the sound was at the right intensity – as disturbing a sight to Thomas as that of a corpse on the embalmer's slab adjusting its own wrappings – and lay back under the lamp.

Thomas tried to clear his mind and concentrate on the picture in front of him. He worked out, as one would work a thorn out of a finger after a day's pruning, the feeling of resentment and jealousy occasioned by his suspicion. The notes were clearly genuine, and showed that Born was not going to use them to pre-empt his own article, which was now, after the afternoon's negotiations, to be delivered at an international conference and published prominently in a leading journal. He had organized it well, he felt, and went over the details in his head, watching Born as he settled into the surface of the couch and prepared to enter the hallucinatory field again, under his mind's suggestion.

Seeing the poster on the departmental notice-board had been a piece of luck: he must have walked past it a dozen times since it had gone up, and never taken more than a glance at it. The poster announced that there was to be a Conference on Psychical Research at which delegates had been invited to speak, but which presented visitors with the opportunity of joining in discussions and participating in the seminars. He checked at the information desk: yes, the seminars were open to all comers, with a registration fee payable to the faculty of eleven pounds a day, a bit steep but they had to print the programmes, didn't they, and hire the rooms – and after all, it was reclaimable against expenses.

He took the printed list of lectures and addresses, papers on all matters encircling the subject, from the President's Welcoming Remarks on Day 1 (already past) to the Round Table Debate winding up the conference, entitled *Where Do We Go From Here?* He found the name of the conference organizer and the address of his office, in one of the rooms of his own college, and went there at once, hoping he would not bump into Born on the way. Born had been in a funny frame of mind all afternoon, and his own hangover hadn't helped, what with all that burgundy and stuff. Doesn't do to mix your drinks, and spirits on top of that was asking for trouble. Still, a thirty-minute lie-down had shifted the worst of it, and this good news brightened him up still further.

Born's hands, clenched tight before, had opened loosely, but his breathing showed he was awake. Didn't seem to be so much watching as listening. Funny how he'd never thought of asking if he heard anything. Too busy getting the details of the visions. That ought to knock them sideways at the conference. That really ought to sweep the floor. With the notebooks and the drawings he shouldn't have too much trouble putting a case together. Bring Born along as well? Give them a demonstration? Probably not advisable, not at this stage. Wait till it had made a stir, then they'd both be toted off around the circuit. London, California . . . Thomas daydreamed, with visions of welcoming committees, of breathless halls of students and their professors hanging on his every word.

Still, back to earth, the conference office had done its best to help, couldn't have been more enthusiastic actually, especially when he pointed out that it would make him the only member of the college to be participating, if they'd let him, and that his talk would follow on well from what had gone before. That was the odd thing about these privately arranged affairs: so often the people most interested might be living on the very doorstep, and still be the last to hear about it. All because of the fragmentation between the disciplines. So now . . .

So now he had a provisional engagement for the last day of the conference but one, the nice middle-of-the-afternoon spot when they'd worked off most of their lunch and weren't starting to fret about their tea. Dear God in heaven, that meant only two days to get the stuff in order. Which would mean abstracting Born's file of notes for an hour or two and running it through the photocopier. He'd have to come up with a scheme to deal with that one. Might just be easiest to . . .

And then this afternoon's discussion, purely fortuitous, while he was waiting to make a confirmatory phone-call, with that anthropologist in the tea-room, who turned out to know all about Aztec mirrors and what they were used for, and who would be speaking at the conference as well. He had told him, over a cup of tea, that none of the facts in Wiston's catalogue told you anything practical about the mirror itself: all that nonsense about who owned what and gave it to whom, when all you needed was a user's guide, an owner's handbook, to tell you how to work the thing. Just like a car, really, he'd rather have the service-manual than the log-book any day.

Thomas had seen the anthropologist before around the college but had never spoken to him: American he must have been, but not a bit abrasive, name of Weiss if he remembered rightly, spent years pottering around in Yucatan or some such place investigating the relics of the old Mexicans, not the modern Spaniards and half-breeds but the real Indians, Aztecs and Mixtecs and Olmecs or what was left of them, who had still preserved remnants of the old cults, and he was now working on pre-Columbian artefacts in the British Museum, commuting up to London three days a week. Nice to meet someone you could talk to straight away, with none of that British stuff-and-nonsense about reticence and introductions. There was a piece of luck if you like. Pity he couldn't let Born into the secret just at present, but he'd save it up for a surprise.

He had a lot to say, Weiss the anthropologist, once you got him going. All the stone mirrors were in Europe now, brought over by the Conquistadores (and you could tell what Weiss thought of them), and had only survived at all because you couldn't melt them down and turn them into crucifixes or doubloons, being made of obsidian, which doesn't do much in the way of melting, not at ordinary temperatures.

But although the stone mirrors had gone, the cults had continued, and instead of the priests having the run of things and sacrificing herds of human victims to their god – he had the name on a scrap of paper: Tezcatlipoca, that was it – by ripping out their hearts with obsidian daggers, they sat around waiting for the next anthropologist to come and ask them silly questions in his Yanqui accent. This time, though, the medicine-man had taken a shine to him, and instead of telling him to run away and play in the jungle, he had given him a live stone, that was right, a live stone, and made him look at it until he couldn't see anything else. This took upwards of five years, and in the meantime he had asked some more questions about the words they used, all the mumbo-jumbo of the ancient rites, and found out that although their mirrors had gone, their names remained in the ritual language – the smoking mirror, the glass to look in, the water-stone, the dark moon, the sun at evening, the stone that cuts, the mask, the wizard-stone, the youth, the night-sign and the jewelled fowl – that mimicked those in the old manuscripts, the *Codex Borbonicus* and the *Popol Vuh*. Fossils they were, just as if all the crosses and reliquaries, croziers and altar-pieces, crucifixes and the very name of Christ had gone, leaving nothing but a bundle of uncouth names and outlandish sayings, about the Tree of Jesse and the Holy Rood, the Eagle, the Day-Star and the First and Last.

'And what did the medicine-men say when you told them the mirrors were alive and well and living in Bloomsbury, safe and sound in the British Museum, along with the Ashanti's Golden Stool and the Elgin Marbles?' Well, they wanted them back, of course they did, not to keep in a museum, but to use, and also to stop them falling into the wrong hands . . . And they had asked him, naturally, since he was going to London, if he would kindly fetch them back, and so he was expected to bring the mirrors, next time he returned. Which might cause problems when he went back . . . But to ask a museum official to restore an object to its original owners and for its original purpose – one might as soon suggest that the great sacrificial pyramid should be raised up again in Tenochtitlan, that the priests should abandon their cassocks and croziers, sharpen their obsidian knives, rip breasts and tear out hearts again, though knowing some priests . . .

So Thomas had asked him, conversationally, what the anthropologist had seen in the live stone that had kept him for five years, staring at a pebble? Nothing was the answer, and when the medicine-man had asked him, he had told him the same: that he saw no more in the stone than he could see in himself, and at that, the medicine-man took the stone and threw it away on the pebble beach – and there he had been thinking it was the talisman that would give him the secret of the universe, the key to all knowledge, the wisdom of the gods.

Well, he should get his doctorate out of it, if nothing else.

And after he had thrown away the stone he had seen what the mirror-cult was all about: you stare at the mirror and hope to see the whole world laid out before you, but all you see is what you see in any other mirror, if you put your face to the glass. The anthropologist showed Thomas a passage in a book: *Thus from the shape beheld in the seer's mirror, Tezcatlipoca came to be regarded as the seer. That into which the wizard gazed became so closely identified with sorcery as to be thought of as wizard-like itself; for Tezcatlipoca is, above all the Mexican deities, the one most nearly connected with the wizard's art. He is* par excellence *the nocturnal god who haunts the crossways and appears in a myriad phantom guises to the night-bound wayfarer. 'These,' says Sahagun, 'were masks that Tezcatlipoca assumed to frighten the people.' He wears the symbol of night upon his forehead; he is the moon, ruler of the night, the wizard who veils himself behind the clouds . . .*

But now, as Thomas was trying to understand what this might mean, he saw a change in the way Born was lying on the couch, and that his legs were straightening and bending and his arms were flexing, and that his blind face under the white eyepieces and between the headphones was writhing and twisting as if a heavy hand with fingers of stone had gripped it hard and was trying to pull it off his skull. The tongue stuck out, and foam appeared at the corners of the lips, which grinned as if being torn apart by a thumb in each corner. He was crying out, but Thomas could not make out the words, though they were the same words repeated again and again.

Thomas bent over Born and jammed his pencil between his teeth, tenderly lifted off the headphones and the clinging eyepieces, laid him on the floor and covered him with a rug.

Then, not knowing what else to do, he told Wiston later, he got down on his knees and started to pray. After a while the writhing subsided, and the noises died away. Born slept, and Thomas stayed beside him on his knees. After a while, he was not sure how long, he felt a hand on his shoulder, and looked up into Born's face, which was empty and hollow and white as a piece of bone.

'God, you didn't half give me a fright,' said Thomas. 'I think I ought to tell you, you've just had an epileptic fit.'

Born burst into tears, and wept like a small child. Wiston could hear him from his room.

# Chapter 16

Born sent one of the porters to Wiston's rooms the following morning with a letter he had written and a cassette he had recorded. The letter asked him to keep the cassette as he was planning to go up to London and did not want it to fall into Thomas's hands.

'He's not looking so good,' said the porter. 'Been overtaxing himself these past few days, if you ask me. Had his light on all night, wouldn't let his bedmaker in, just stuck his head round the door and gave her this for you, sir.'

Wiston thanked him, and wrote a short note for him to take back, asking Born to come round for a spot of lunch, if he felt well enough. He thought it was the least he could do, if the latter days had been proving too much of a strain. And he had something for Born to do. Then he opened Born's letter and read it.

'Dear Wiston, I have sent this cassette for you to keep, if you will, as I shall be going up to London to do a little more reading in the British Library, and also to avoid Thomas and his sessions for a day or so. The concentrated effort seems to have affected my health slightly, so I think it would be as well for me to keep out of the way. Yours, John Born.'

It was plain to Wiston, from what Born wrote to his mother that morning, that he had gone to bed after his attack, and he could not have let Thomas call a doctor or made any other arrangements to seek medical attention. Thomas had very little to say about this to Wiston later, and seemed to think that if he had acted sooner, Born's death might have been averted. Wiston did not think so: everything happened after Born's fit with such extraordinary rapidity that he could not see how even Thomas's most sedulous attentions could have deflected the crisis. However, he did nothing to prevent Thomas from thinking that he might have stopped the whole thing, if only he had telephoned for a doctor or an ambulance when Born was first taken ill. But, as Thomas told him, Born recovered so quickly after his first haggard return to consciousness that he was able to persuade him not to make a fuss about it.

Born wrote to his mother:

'I am afraid I have been feeling rather ill for the last couple of days, with the classic symptoms of academic overtiredness – shivering, yawning, dozing off at odd moments, generally feeling under the weather. The strain of the last couple of sessions with Thomas has gone beyond a joke, and I'm sorry to say I frightened him badly by passing out on him through sheer exhaustion, towards the end of an hour-and-a-half long séance. I wouldn't worry about this at all. I'm going up to London for a day's work in the British Library, which will give me plenty of time to sit quietly and relax – if only on the train!

'Thomas seems to think that I am trying to push him out of the limelight (not that there is any) over the séances, and I don't want him to think I am holding information back from him or stringing him along. So I am anxious to let him have all the facts he needs in case he wants to start writing up – there's no shortage of data – and there may even be some details you can help with, about family medical history. I am trying to get a copy of my own medical records out of the hospital, but they seem reluctant to let me have one. Thomas may write you a questionnaire, as I'm hopeless at remembering family details of the kind he needs – insanity, nervous disorders, migraine, fits, epilepsy, sleepwalking and so on. I must say I can't remember anything of the sort (not that I'm sure I'd want to) but if you can, and could pass it on, it would be all used confidentially: no names, no pack-drill. Hallucination, that was another thing. I know it sounds inquisitive, but Thomas wants to get as much information as he can about his subject (me) before he does any writing. I'm only sorry he hasn't asked me to help him with it, as co-authoring an article, even for a scientific journal, would be rather a joy.

'Why don't you come over before the end of the vacation? It's getting to the time of year when people start disappearing to the other end of the earth, and a weekend with you here would do wonders to bridge the gap before the beginning of term. I've got to the stage of looking in the mirror for company, and not liking what I see . . .! So I hope you'll find time to come up. Until then, goodbye and all my love. John.'

A brave letter, Wiston thought, as much for its barefaced, helpless deceitfulness as for what it left unwritten. This the cassette supplied. As soon as the porter had gone, Wiston played it through on his little machine. As he pressed the green button to start the tape, he noticed that Born was standing at his window and staring across the court, and felt tempted to wave to him: he would have seen the wave, Wiston was sure, and it might have cheered him up. But Born would be coming round for lunch within three hours, so he did not bother.

Wiston later transcribed the tape, and added his own comments where he thought them necessary. It began abruptly.

'Suddenly into the field, and it is a field, a great field, a mile across or more, and a great tall tree, rotten and hollow, and the grass around it withered and burnt, and lightning continually striking the tree, and water spilling around the roots from a cleft in its side. And the voice behind me saying, go forward, and I go forward to the trunk of the tree, and the voice says, reach in with your hand, and take out what you find there. And I see it within the hollow of the tree, the dark moon, the black mirror, and I touch it with my hand, and its face is cold. And the voice saying, take it out, but do not look at your face in its face, or in mine. And I withdraw my hand, and immediately the sides of the tree close together, and the tree is whole, though it is blasted, and my arm is held at the wrist. And still I see the mirror within the tree, shining very brightly with the moon in its face. And the voice at my back saying, you will come to me, and you will do as I will: you will bring the mirror into my hand, and you will tell me what you see there. And it was not his voice, but another's and I was afraid.

'And then out of the tree comes a loud voice saying, do not go, do not take it, rather cut off your hand and leave it within me, but do not give it to him. And he who was standing behind me reaches out his hand and strikes the tree, and the tree cries out, and my hand is held more tightly from within. And he shows me a knife, its blade in the trunk, and the knife is of a black stone like the mirror. And he says, if you will, cut off your hand, but if you will not, bring me the mirror. And I say, if I bring it to you, what will you give me? And he says, look in its face, and what you see, that will I give you.

'And the face of the mirror that was within the trunk of the tree grew dark, and then a light fell upon it, and in that light I saw I was standing upon a very high place, and all around me were rich farmlands, and I was very glad when I saw them, and said to him, these are yours to give me? And he said, if you will give me the mirror, they are yours. And the tree wept again, and said, cut off your hand, but do not give him the mirror, for you will lose your life. And he who stood behind me said, you are already dead, and looking down I saw that my arm was white bone from the shoulder to the wrist, where it went into the trunk of the tree.

'But he said, your hand will be restored, and your life with it, and again I looked into the stone and saw the ruins of a church, with its tower still standing, and from behind me he spoke to me and said, go inside, and I saw myself within the ruins of the church, and he stood at my back. Look up, he said, and read what is written on the wall of the tower, and I saw my name carved upon a stone set into the wall, in deep letters, with the dates of my birth and death. Then he said to me, Climb, and I found a stone stair in the tower, and climbed it until I reached the top, and still I stood before the tree with my hand trapped within its trunk. And the tower was higher than it seemed, and higher than the high place. And when I looked down there was a great city and many people coming and going to and from their business, and the one that stood behind me said, cast yourself down, and your angels will catch you as you fall, if you will draw the mirror out of the tree, and give it into my hand, and tell me what you see there. And the angels flew to and fro below me in the air, and their wings were burnt, for the lightning continued to play, and their faces were blackened and scorched and their feathers singed, and the stench of their burning came up to me as I stood upon the tower. And their faces were the faces of demons.

'And the voice from within the tree said the third time, do not give him the mirror, rather cut off your hand and leave it within the trunk of the tree, and you will save your life, and go free.'

*(Up to this point the narrative, delivered in the 'tonic voice', continues quite calmly, as if reading from a prepared script, though one printed carelessly on old paper in an unfamiliar face, perhaps black-letter. The details seem to be a curious singling-out of subject matter from Dee's own relations and the Gospel account of the Temptation in the Wilderness. At this point, though, a change occurs in the voice.)*

'And I looked into the stone a third time, and I was upon a stony beach, and a forest was at my back, with palms and great trees that dropped their roots from their branches into the water. And an old man sat beside me, and I could not see his face. He asked me, do you wish to know the secret of eternal life? If so, take this stone and look at it, and tell me what you see. And he gave me the fragment of a stone, black, with one face smooth. It is a live stone, he said, it has lived and it will live and it is living now. And I knew his voice, but could not see his face. So I took the stone and held it in my hand and looked at it, and sat there longer than I can tell, with the stone in my hand, and it was a live stone.'

*(Looking at this in retrospect, there seems a great affinity between this vision and Thomas's daydreaming, which occurred so far as one can tell concurrently with the vision (in itself a remarkable thing) and this would indicate that Thomas's thoughts were being transmitted in some way across the room. But the great vividness of Born's telling of the story, in spite of the archaisms, makes it seem to come from some more direct source than Thomas, who had only heard the story casually from a man he met in a café. In Thomas's version of the story the*

*anthropologist (who had been replaced by Born himself) spent five years in Mexico listening to the maunderings of a guru from the Stone Age of the country, giving a pseudo-philosophy of meditation on an object until it revealed the personality of the meditator. At the end, the stone was thrown back on to the beach as a thing of no value. But as Born's narrative continues, this parallel becomes less and less clear, and new details are given that change the story completely.)*

'I have written to my mother, I will write to Wiston, and Thomas will hear the story from him, and from these notes. I fear I am going mad, and that I will go mad unless these visions stop. I cannot see a reflective surface without . . . under it . . . something . . . blacker than . . . and deeper than . . . the object's own depth (*which, being true of all reflecting surfaces, is not such an odd observation*) but at least there the walls will be white, and the beds will be white, and they will bring me white flowers, and even the blades of the knives will be white, so that I cannot see . . . my face in them.

'And now the ground all about the tree has come up with green grass as high as my calf, and the ground has taken up all the water that flowed out of the tree. And the voice behind me told me, look into the stone that you hold in your hand, and tell me what you see. And I was on a beach with a black stone in my hand that shone like glass. And there was a man before me on the beach, and he held a great flat stone before him on the sand, and was smoothing it and grinding it with another stone he held in his hand. And the stone I held was of the stone he had before him, and he asked me, what do you see in the stone? And I said, nothing that is not within myself. And he took the stone from me and cast it upon the beach, where it lay among the other stones and I could not tell it from them. And he said, Look then, on this stone, and he held it to my face. And there was a great cry behind me, and the cry came from the tree, and the tree was behind me. And my arm was free and whole, and he stood before me with the stone in his hands, and he said, Come and see.

'And I covered my face with my hands, and he said again, Come and see, and tell me what it is that you have seen. And I bent my head, and covered my face with my hands. And he cried again, Come and see, and stretched out his hand and grasped my face, and a voice in the tree cried out again, and the tree fell, and the grass withered, and it was night. And I said, I will not come, I will not see. And he cried in a loud voice, Because you have not come, because you have not seen, your promise is broken. Go from me and do not return; your life has ended and you will see no more. And I raised my hands to my face, and the skull was bare bone, and I had no eyes to see nor ears to hear, and all was dark and silent. And a voice was singing in the darkness, and I woke.'

*I shall not play this tape to Thomas, and I shall not play it again. After I had transcribed it, I erased it, and over it, to wipe it out completely, I recorded some English songs that were playing on the radio, some of those that Born had wanted to sing, and those I made him sing. For the voices on the tape were voices I knew: Born spoke with his own voice, and the voice in the tree was familiar too, but I did not hear it again, only heard it reported to me. And the third voice was my own.*

# Chapter 17

Before Born arrived for what was to be an early lunch, Wiston went out to the shops with a carrier-bag to buy food for the meal, simple provisions that he could put together without help from the college kitchens. He remembered their picnic in the churchyard with some pleasure, in spite of the disappointment of the sale, and hoped, if Born were well enough, to have that pleasure again, indoors and in different circumstances.

Wiston chose the food carefully and, though he detested anything done to a theme, whether a meal, a concert or a fancy-dress ball, he tried to find items that were black and shining. A little delicatessen near the cinema yielded black lump-fish roe that would do well enough for caviare, and black olives in a polystyrene pot with the price scrawled on the lid. In the market he found black grapes that tasted of strawberries, with fine skins whose bloom would wash off with a little water. White curd cheese would go well with black pumpernickel bread, for which he had to make a second visit to the grocer's, and strong black coffee, continental-roast, would finish off the meal.

He returned to his room and arranged the food neatly on the table, then went into his study to wait for Born to arrive: the court was visible, reflected in the mirror behind the square piano, so he would not be taken by surprise. The study, in daylight, was a pleasanter room than at night, though Wiston preferred it after dark, and the sunlight shone prettily in the reflecting surfaces and glanced strongly off the mirror into Wiston's eyes. He could see Born coming diagonally across the court, and felt in the lining of his pocket for the twist of Born's hair to rub between his fingers; but the sunlight dazzled him, and he drew a cloth across the mirror.

Born, as he approached, seemed alert and oddly light on his feet, as if he had been purged to lose weight. There was a fragility about him: as Wiston watched him crossing the court he had seemed to sway a little with the wind. The illusion was heightened by his master's gown which, worn over a dark suit and a black tie, made him look as if he had dressed for the funeral of a near relation.

Resigned to a monochromatic luncheon, Wiston changed his over-cheerful jacket for a darker one in black velvet that he wore in his study on winter evenings to keep the draughts away, and opened the door an instant before Born could knock.

'Come in.'

'You found my tape?'

'I have played it through, but I don't suppose you want to talk about it.' This was not a question, and Born did not answer. Instead, he looked towards the table and then glanced away. His eyes still had the rings of darkness around them that Thomas had noticed before; but apart from these shadows and a certain pallor there was nothing about his appearance that would make anyone stop him, sit him down and offer to fetch a doctor, or tea, or brandy. Except, perhaps, that he had not shaved.

'I didn't think you'd have much of an appetite, so I went out and got a few light bits and pieces that should do to keep body and soul together.'

Born grinned pallidly. Wiston remembered the picnic-party not so long before, and wished he had a bottle of wine for Born to uncork, to give his hands something to do. He cut the pumpernickel into thin slices with a black-handled butcher's knife, and made some remark about bread being bad for the keenness of the edge.

'You should sharpen it on your shoe,' said Born, and took the knife from Wiston, handle first. He lifted one shoe – Wiston noticed that the black leather had not seen polish for a week or more – and stroked the knife back and forth across the welt. Then he wiped the blade, tried it on the fine hairs at his wrist, and gave it back. Wiston, taken aback at this performance, said nothing, but washed the knife and cut more bread and butter until the plate was full, then offered it to Born.

Born ate sparingly of the lump-fish roe, the olives and the grapes, and clumsily, as several of the small round black shining objects fell on to the tablecloth and rolled about, but he plastered his bread with the white curd cheese and ate as if it had been as good for his soul as communion wafers. Wiston enjoyed watching him, and did so between mouthfuls: he himself had developed a ravenous appetite, and the sparse fare on the table was not enough to satisfy him. Wiston noticed that the reason Born dropped his food was quite simple: he was not looking at it.

'Tell me, Born,' said Wiston, 'are you seeing things?'

'What do you mean?'

'Outside the experiment, outside the Ganzfeld, do you have visions?'

'Not all the time.'

'When you look at black reflecting surfaces?'

'You got that off the cassette.'

'No, from watching you eat. What can you see if you stare at that olive, that grape? What will you do if I bring you a black coffee and an After Eight?'

Born managed another grin, and swallowed like Thomas with a mouthful of spines.

'I'll look the other way.'

'You don't like what you see?'

Born swallowed again, but did not smile.

'I'd do anything . . .'

'Would you do what I tell you?'

'Yes.'

'No quibbling, no provisos about within reason or out of reason?'

Born nodded.

'I think a coffee would do you good. Can you face it milkless? There isn't a drop in the house.'

'I'll drink it with my eyes shut, if you'll risk my spilling it on the floor.'

Wiston smiled and went to put the volcanic Italian percolator on the gas-ring. Born stood at the window, looking across the court to his own room. *We make a comical pair,* Wiston thought, *robed in black like court conjurors, meddling with dark potions and stills.* He waited for the water to boil.

'You can tolerate window-glass, then?'

'Yes, if it's clear, with the light behind it.'

'But not puddles, or shop-fronts, or hearses, or patent-leather shoes, or black enamel?'

Born drummed his fists lightly on the radiator.

'Not if I can avoid them.'

'And do you recognize what is the source of this neurotic obsession?'

'I'm not sure.'

'It's easy to see where it stems from.'

'Where?'

'From your rivalry with Thomas. Your insecurity in the college. Your childhood, your mother, your every weakness of character, all focused into one simple thing, a refusal to look yourself in the face.'

Wiston thought this schoolmasterly summing-up, this end-of-term report, would be platitudinous enough to annoy Born into answering, and he paused for effect.

'I'm waiting for an answer, Born.'

Born was silent. Wiston tucked his thumbs into his lapels, rocked on his toes and continued.

'Now the way to deal with this kind of neurosis, this morbid obsession that threatens to spread further and further – and will spread, if you do not control it now – is to confine it to a single object in which you can concentrate all your fear, all your disquiet, all your nightmares and bad, waking dreams.'

The volcano erupted coffee, and Wiston poured out two cups.

'Come into the study, would you?'

Born followed like Bluebeard's last wife, as if he expected to find the walls hung with mirrors, each filled with a wilderness of visions. But there was only one mirror on the wall, and that was draped with a cloth.

Born sat on a hard chair and sipped his coffee, eyes averted.

Wiston went on with his analysis.

'Now if you had developed a morbid fear of cars, because you had been overtaken dangerously in the past and driven off the road, and this fear had spread to every car you saw, you might reduce your fear by picking one car, investing it with the essence of car-ness, and letting it contain all the horror in itself. Wouldn't that be better than going in fear and trembling of the whole breed of cars?'

'Yes, I suppose it would.'

'And you could then face all the cars in creation without losing your nerve?'

Born nodded.

'And then it wouldn't be long before you saw that there was nothing to choose between the one monstrous car and the millions of others on the roads, and your neurosis would disappear completely. No more fear, no more terror, no more cowering at the sound of a hooter or the flash of headlamps over the horizon.'

'No.'

'But before you reached that happy state, wouldn't it be better if the beast or its image were out of the way?'

'How do you mean?'

'Well, for instance, if you'd chosen a car like Thomas's Ford Escort, say, there would always be the chance of meeting it, or one like it, at any moment.'

'I'm beginning to see . . .'

'But if you picked a veteran Daimler in a motor-museum, you'd be unlikely ever to see it again, unless you went out of your way to seek it out, on a mission of morbid curiosity.'

'That sounds quite convincing.'

'The mirror that is causing all the trouble, if I am not mistaken, is a certain one in the Renaissance Gallery of the British Museum, Doctor Dee's obsidian mirror, the devil's looking-glass we've heard so much about.'

'Well, only the photograph . . .'

'You've never seen the looking-glass itself?'

'Never.'

'Let us do the obvious thing. That is the one real mirror, the only one that matters. All other mirrors are merely shadows. You haven't shaved today.'

'I'm sorry.'

'Quite understandable. Do you think you could face going into the bathroom and dealing with your bristles? Use my round shaving-glass.'

'I'll have a try.'

'Good. You'll find it in the cabinet with a brush, soap and a disposable razor.'

Born went into the bathroom. Wiston heard the door of the cabinet open and shut, water run into the basin, the slapping of the lathered brush and the stridulation of the razor against rough skin. He sat still and listened. More running water – cold, he guessed – and the rubbing of a towel. Born came back into the room. Wiston stared at his chin, where a bead of blood was forming. *There is no mirror in the cabinet,* he thought, *nor one in the bathroom at all.*

'For a blind shave with a fresh blade, that was pretty good. Just one slight nick on your chin and a patch of stubble on your left cheek.'

Born laughed aloud.

*A good performance,* thought Wiston, *and showed a lot of nerve.*

'Go to the mirror on the wall and take the cloth away.'

Born shook his head.

'Do as I say.'

Born shook his head again. Wiston went to the open keyboard, and played a short phrase, a phrase he would remember, the tune of the song in the garden.

Born lowered his head and went to the mirror. He reached up, took the cloth by two corners and lifted it off.

'Tell me what you see there.'

Born shook his head again. Wiston saw in the reflection that his eyes were shut, clenched tight. He played the phrase again, and Born opened his eyes, his face contorted, and rushed to the open window as if he wanted to dash himself on to the cobblestones two floors below.

Wiston went behind him and gripped his shoulders hard.

'Don't do that,' he said gently. 'Just tell me what you saw.'

'I saw . . . you. I saw . . . your face.'

'Of course you did. I was standing behind you.'

Born shook his head and gripped the windowsill. Wiston covered the glass, and turned Born round to face the room again. He stood with his head bowed, the blood smeared across his chin. Wiston spoke to him.

'What you will do is this. I shall phone the director of the gallery where the mirror is on display: he's an old and close friend of mine. I shall tell him that one of my colleagues wishes to inspect the mirror, for academic reasons, and I shall concoct some tale about collaborative work. I'm not sure why I'm doing all this. He will take you up to the gallery after the main museum closes. You will wait in the Reading Room, and work there until the time. You have a reader's ticket, of course.'

Born nodded.

'It is important, vitally important, that when he takes the mirror out of the case he lets you hold it, even if only for a moment. Say you want to look at the back, check it for inscriptions, damage, whatever you like. Use your imagination. But take it in your hands. Look at it hard, make sure you have the light on your face, and remember what you see. I shall want to hear about it when you come back.'

Born bowed his head.

'The train leaves at two o'clock, and it will get you to King's Cross by three-thirty. Go to the British Museum on foot. It will take you twenty minutes, and the walk will clear your head. Then do an hour's work in the Reading Room. At five-fifteen you will go to the entrance-hall, and the curator will be waiting for you at the foot of the stairs. All this is necessary, believe me, for your sanity. These states of mind cannot be cured by conventional methods. The only way is to do what I tell you.'

Born listened in silence, without moving. Wiston continued.

'I must say I feel rather responsible. I may have precipitated this crisis without thinking. Lending you that catalogue may have been a mistake. I shouldn't have made such a fuss at the sale. And I should never have interfered in your work with Thomas. I feel very guilty about all this, and feel I owe you some help. We have an arrangement of a sort, after all. It isn't as if one could just stand idly by.'

Born smiled, and moved his lips as if about to speak or – thought Wiston fancifully – sing. Then he released the windowsill and came towards him, his hand stretched out.

'Thanks for all your help,' he said. 'I'll see you when I get back.'

'You'll do as I said?'

'I'll try to.'

'Do try.'

Born left the room, his gown loose about his shoulders and his head down.

Wiston went to the telephone, and dialled the number of the British Museum.

# Chapter 18

Wiston came to a satisfactory arrangement over the phone with the museum curator – who was surprised that Born had not conducted his own negotiations – and when he had finished, went into the court for a little fresh air. He had only made one circuit of the grass-plots when Thomas, mopping his face with his handkerchief and with one pocket-lining hanging out of his jacket, rushed up to him and seized him by the arm.

'I'm worried about Born,' he said, like a character in a soap opera.

'Trouble at the lab?' asked Wiston.

'He's just been to see you.'

'I had him to lunch, as a matter of fact. He left ten minutes ago.'

'You didn't notice anything funny about him?'

'Nothing seemed particularly wrong with him, if that's what you mean. He may have looked paler, tenser than usual, but nothing dramatic. Why do you ask?'

'I had a full-blown epileptic fit on my hands last night. Scared me out of my wits. Didn't know what to do.'

'Did you call a doctor?'

'No, it was all over before there was much I could do, except stick a pencil in his mouth. Look at it.' He produced the pencil: it was bitten almost through. *Ten points for First Aid*, thought Wiston, looking at the pencil with distaste, *and thank your stars you didn't try the Kiss of Life: he'd have bitten off your tongue at the root*. He replied:

'Born said nothing to me about it, nothing at all.'

'You didn't think he was behaving oddly?'

'Not beyond what might be caused by sitting up all night and tampering with the subconscious in the irresponsible fashion you have been promoting. Don't you think you might have gone too far? Tipped him over the edge?'

Thomas looked thoughtful, and shuffled his feet in the grass.

'It didn't occur to you that by concentrating your hypnotic efforts on one person you might run the risk of brainwashing him? Or bringing out some hidden weakness? He told me about your sessions, and I don't like the sound of them at all.'

'What don't you like?'

'Born having visions and you taking notes.'

'What's your objection to that?'

'It's too much like an inquisition. He's bound to tell you what you want to hear.'

'He tells me what he's seen, and writes it down in his diary. Then I check the one against the other.'

'Could I see the diary? Or look at your notes? You're thinking of publishing very shortly, I believe.'

'I'm reading a paper at the seminar tomorrow, part of the psychical research conference they're holding here.'

'You've written the paper?'

'It's with the typist now.'

'And the conference organizers have vetted it?'

'I've given them a draft.'

'And it contains everything Born told you about his visions?'

'All the relevant details.'

'I'm afraid he may have led you up the garden path. You see, he's suffering from a set of paranoid delusions which drive him into extravagant fantasies on the one hand, and persecution mania on the other. He has combined the two with . . . the results you have seen.'

Thomas, unspeaking, led Wiston to his study, where Born's diary and his own notes lay on the table with the remains of his elevenses and a sticky jar of marmalade. One of the curtains was still drawn, and the little light there was had been filtered through the leaves of pot plants and reflected off the faded upholstery. There was a steady throbbing from the boiler in the basement, and Wiston felt the dull vibrations rising through the soles of his feet.

Thomas had bought a Tretchikoff print from Woolworth's and hung it over the fireplace: a Korean girl with mustard-yellow skin standing against a background of lime-green forest foliage and palm trees. Her turquoise kimono was fastened at the shoulder by three cornelian buttons, a detail that afflicted Wiston throughout the conversation. He wrinkled his nose, and sniffed the musty air.

Thomas opened the diary and let Wiston see the pages Born had written. He read them carefully twice through, and closed the green-backed notebook. Thomas looked at him, his mouth open.

'It's the old division, between you, the scientists, and us, the artists. You, as a scientist, could see no point in historical research, even when it was clear you were dealing with an object with a history.'

'The mirror?'

'The mirror. Do you know whose mirror?'

'From what I could read of the catalogue, any number of people's.'

'If I told you that one of its owners, Dr John Dee, a mathematician, soothsayer and alchemist at the court of Elizabeth I, used it for the same purpose as you, would that jog your mind?'

'I'm not sure I follow you.'

'Dee wanted to use the mirror like a crystal ball, to communicate with spirits. He found he could see nothing in it with his own eyes, so he called on a man named Kelly. Kelly had some reputation as a seer, a speculator, a crystal-gazer, a medium. He was also, like most mediums, a calculating and unrepentant fraud. He'd had his ears cropped in the pillory for a similar offence, and came to a bad end. I am sorry to say that Dee, the greatest natural philosopher and experimental scientist of his time, was taken in by him completely.'

'You mean old Born's been stringing me along?'

'Work it out for yourself. What was in it for him? Why go through this rigmarole, waste a whole summer's vacation, unless to get his own back for some imaginary injury?'

Thomas shook his head like a man unused to mistrusting his friends.

'He worried you into writing up before your time by making you think he would beat you to it. You didn't want to show him your conclusions. So he decided, then or earlier, to spin you a yarn. He knew you'd never notice: you hadn't read the books. So he told you a picturesque story conjured up out of his researches – you never asked what he was doing all day in the library, did you? – and you thought you had beamed it all to him on some psychic radio-wave.'

'What's he doing now, for God's sake?'

'If he went to London, he'll have gone to the British Library which, I don't need to remind you, occupies the same set of buildings as the British Museum. They have the whole collection there among the manuscripts: all Dee's diaries, papers, documents, most of them unpublished. If you could make head or tail of them, they'd remind you of this.' Wiston tapped the notebook. 'Men in tall hats, sea voyages, secret conclaves, it's all in there. He'll be getting on to alchemy and the transmutation of metals next, then wife-swapping and necromancy at the court of the Holy Roman Emperor. You could read it yourself.'

'You needn't sound so bloody pleased. You put him up to it, you did. You must have done. Bloody academic conspiracies, they make me sick. What am I supposed to do now? There's that seminar tomorrow, they've seen my notes, and I'm supposed to be reading this to them. What a laugh. Scientist Trips Over Guinea-Pig's Tale. All over the Sunday papers and bang goes my career.'

Wiston was sorry that Thomas could think of nothing but preferment: where had his concern for Born gone now?

'Nothing of the sort has happened. There has been no conspiracy. Though you were right about one thing, but for the wrong reasons.'

'Right about what, may I ask?'

'Born's mental health. The balance of his mind has become quite seriously deranged. He has started to suffer from quite genuine hallucinations.'

'Oh yes, all faked up like his epileptic fit. Very convincing, I'm sure.'

'That fit was perfectly real. He had another in my rooms, at lunch time.'

'He had a fit and you sent him up to London? You need putting away, you do.'

'He wanted to go. What was I to do? Lock him in his room?' Wiston felt that Thomas was with him now, and would do what he said. Now he could lecture him, browbeat him, even flatter him a little, and Thomas would agree. The boiler vibrated, and the Korean girl leered from the wall.

'Of course you realize now what is happening? Born becomes obsessed with the miror, and the obsession drives him to do things he would not otherwise have done. Terrible things. You are a scientist. Your universal order will accommodate anomalies that seem absurd to the layman, but Born is a pure logician: he has nothing like your knowledge to protect him. He is an agnostic to your Inquisition. You give him irrational experiences, hallucinations, states of madness and mental chaos, and he has nothing to guard himself against them. Spiritually, intellectually, you unbalance his mind. He needs a stable world, without irrational elements in nature. He is logical, reasoning, sceptical of faith, and you send voices into his ears, visions before his eyes, and he can make no sense of them. And when he tries to put some order to them, he hangs them on the framework of a well-known tale, a romance taken out of the history books, one you would not recognize but which would let him off the horror of admitting what it was he really saw, that was worse than anything you can possibly imagine. Now he cannot get it out of his head, and sees it all the time.'

'Dear God in Heaven,' said Thomas, and sat down on the floor, his head between his knees. 'Where's he gone to now?'

'That's what you will have to find out. If he is in the British Museum, he could either have gone to the Manuscripts Room, where he will be reading more of Kelly's visions to keep his own under control, or to the Renaissance Gallery where they keep the mirror. God knows what he might do there. I think it is your duty to find out.'

'Why don't you phone them up and tell them what's going on?'

'I'm not certain that anything is going on, but I feel you should be there to make sure. Don't interfere, don't try and stop him, just follow him and watch what he is doing.'

'I'm not going up there to make a fool of myself, mind.' Thomas was beaten.

'More of a fool, you mean? You've done pretty well so far, Master Thomas, and I would love to hear what they'll say to you at the conference and back at your department when this is all over.'

Thomas turned up the palms of both hands and stared at them as if he hoped he would find an answer written there. Wiston had a sudden vision of a small boy in an examination-room, with notes scribbled on his wrist, under his sleeve, and smiled.

'I have a tape.'

Thomas looked up, and probed one nostril with an index finger wrapped in his handkerchief.

'Got a bit of a cold coming on,' he said.

'I have a cassette,' said Wiston. 'Born recorded it over the last few days. He says what it was he really saw. You might find it useful. You could play it to the seminar. I think it would impress them.'

'Where is it then, you – ' Thomas trapped the word.

'Locked away, I'm afraid. You see, I promised to keep it safe for him.'

'That bloody cassette. Dear Christ, and to think it was lying right there in front of my nose, and I didn't – '

Wiston counted up to five with his fingers on the table, feeling them stick to the clammy surface. The boiler throbbed in the basement.

'If you catch him in time, you might . . .'

Thomas crouched on the floor, tearing with his teeth at a strip of skin beside his thumbnail.

'Tell me what I'm supposed to do.'

'Follow him, keep an eye on him. Make sure he doesn't see you. Then . . . it's up to you. If you go now you'll catch the next train. You won't be far behind.'

Wiston watched Thomas take up his wallet and his mackintosh and led him to the door.

'I can find my own way out,' said Thomas, like a visitor in his own room. Wiston blew a kiss to the Korean girl over the fireplace, shut the door and followed close behind him down the stairs.

# Chapter 19

Leaving King's Cross Station by the side-exit, Born hurriedly ducked around the barriers and over Euston Road, flinching as the taxies chugged past, their black sides gleaming malevolently. He found himself in the cool, quiet mesh of streets made up of rooming-houses and private hotels that lies beneath the pinnacled outline of the great turrets of St Pancras' Station. Born left no record of his journey, in letters, journals or tapes, so Wiston later reconstructed it, following the familiar route through the London A to Z.

Passing from the seamier terraces into Judd Street, where the presence of London University begins to loom, Born would have crossed into Hastings Street and found relief in the shady crescent of Cartwright Gardens: he may even have sat for a while to watch the sparrows feeding and the children playing in the dirt. It was after four o'clock, the schools were on holiday, and he was in no hurry. Then, getting up, brushing the seat of his trousers and tucking in his shirt, he would have gone out into the sun again, and walked the length of Marchmont

Street without once looking to right or left at the bookshops, fishmonger's or greengrocer's stalls for fear of dark glass or glossy tiles, cabinets of writhing eels, or piles of aubergines blacked and shining like policemen's boots.

He might have looked at his watch – taking care not to catch his face reflected in the dial – and found time was moving slower than he thought, and that the moment of facing the mirror was not yet. So he may have crossed to the corner of Russell Square and laid his jacket, as the afternoon was hot, over a chair outside the café, and bought coffee and fruit-cake, his last conscious meal, and lingered in the sun between an American in a buttercup-yellow sweatshirt drawn up at the elbows and a Frenchman in blue denim: all matt, benevolent surfaces he could stare into without despair, while he drank his cooling coffee and watched the bees dip their mandibles into the drops of sweet, spilled liquid, brushing them gently away with his fingers as he raised the cup. But not to look into their eyes, or the black eyes of the pigeons frolicking under the falling jet of the fountain, feathers battered by the spray, or at the black badge with the branching white emblem on the Frenchman's lapel, or at the American's black coffee that reflected blue light from the sky.

To get Born safely to the mirror, let the American ask him the time, which he tells him, and then for directions to the British Museum.

'I'm going there myself. We'll have to be quick, though. It's nearly closing time.'

'You think we'll be too late? I've come all this way to look at the terracottas, and now I won't see them? That's too bad.'

'I'm going to use the library, and it doesn't shut till nine.'

'You'll be okay, then. Lucky for you.'

They pass the fountains together and cross the road at the park's far corner, talking of terracotta, and go into Montague Street and along the blind flank of the Museum, then turn left into Great Russell Street beside the gleaming black railings from which Born averts his eyes. In the shop-windows opposite are tartan woollens and works on the Tao, the Tarot and Tai-Ch'i: Born does not look at them, knowing what lies behind the smooth panes of plate-glass. They pass through the great iron gates and walk slowly up to the white portico of newly-washed pillars, the American chattering of tiles and patterned wall-paper, and the huge doors already spitting out the tourist parties and groups of running children. The guard at the top of the steps has a bright black peak to his cap, and his dark eyes peer out from under it, so Born is glad to have nothing to declare, no bags to search, and passes through the doors, across the hall and into the sanctuary of the Reading Room.

He shows his card to a Jamaican girl, keeping his eyes to her unreflecting hair, while she looks at him oddly, but waves him through. Under the great blue dome with its golden letters and mute clockface the echoes chase and tumble, and Born traces the booming to the iron-shod volumes of the catalogue, and the rustling to the scholars as they bob and weave from desk to shelves and back, shuffling slips of paper and clicking ballpoints like insects under a dome of blue sky, carrying books like ants'-eggs to and fro.

Born finds an empty table, and takes his seat. There is a screen in front of him to hide his face, with a multitude of little shelves and ledges, a curious row of bristles and several brass hooks whose purpose is unknown to him – for cleaning dusty fingers, he supposes, or hanging up your hat. He lays a pencil on the table to mark his place, goes to the catalogue, fills in a slip and orders a book to be fetched.

He has to occupy the time remaining, so, with a glance at the clock-face, he leaves the Reading Room again and enters the hall. The friendly American, caught up in a party of tourists, has got no further than the shop, and waves to him with a fan of postcards, but Born does not wave back. A feeling of blackness and melancholy descends; he walks through to the cases of early books and manuscripts that seem to lose their lustre and become dark, sooty-black and indistinct, and the printed pages spread their ink and blur their lettering, so that the cases, glazed over and lit harshly from above, are uniformly dark.

He wanders back across the hall and into the postcard-shop, where the colours are bright and the chiming tills and chattering tourists fill his mind with confusion, and he lets his feet take him, against the general flow, into a realm of monsters, sneering cats and bearded bulls and great lion-chested men on pillars, the gates of Heaven and Hell, strange figures of basalt three times higher than a man.

His head swims and he sits down on a bench, but the bench gives way beneath him, he sinks into it and feels no support, and as he sinks, the hooked bill of a gigantic bird of prey bears down upon him, to peck his skull open and draw out the oozing brain.

Children stop beside him and peer into his face, and he sees the guard coming, so he rises and drags himself to another chamber, where there are figures of men with all their blood drained out of them, their skins as white as marble, wrestling with snakes and wolves, and another where the men are black and scaled like dragons, beaked like eagles, with clawed hands and heavy clubs that glitter like steel, and their hides are as dark as iron plates and shine with a hundred faces. And the hundred faces are one face, the face he has seen before and wants never to see again, and whose voice was the voice from the tree.

And now his book will be fetched, so he goes back to the library and crosses below the dome, the high vault opening into the unfocused blue of the afternoon sky, the thunder rattling and booming. They will not give him his book, but send him down a long gallery with polished walls, where convex mirrors are set to catch him, throwing his face from one to the other, past him, behind him, as the swing doors flap their rubber lips in his face.

He finds himself in the North Library, a pillared refuge as calm and silent as an embalming-chamber in the Valley of the Kings. In return for his slip, they give him a bulky folio in blind-stamped calf, the great book, where the mystery is revealed and the answer given. He takes it to a vacant table and sits down to read.

Faces peer from the gallery, and out of the green lampshades on the desk, but he ignores them, propping the book on a wooden lectern, opening the covers and finding the chapter he must read. But the pages are blank, and over the blankness is a layer of black he cannot penetrate: only the red lines of the pentacle and the rubric show through, and he can read nothing. As he returns the book to the counter, his head clears, and he looks at the clock on the wall: five minutes to his meeting, when the curator will lead him up to the gallery where they keep the mirror, and will bring him before it, face to face.

The faces crowd upon him as he leaves the room: Wiston leers from behind a pillar, the American tries to catch his eye, even the bobbing figure of Thomas lurches towards him across the hall, but he takes no notice and walks calmly on, to the foot of the monumental staircase where a thin, indoor-faced man greets him, shakes him by the hand and leads him up the stairs, chattering excitedly.

But Born cannot hear him, and can only see, in front of his eyes, a disk of blackness growing wider and wider.

# Chapter 20

Thomas arrived at King's Cross Station on the train that followed Born's, and pushed his way through the pedestrian underpass against the rush-hour crowds, emerging from the mouth of the underground station with his face red and his hair on end like the devil in a mystery play. He stopped the third taxi he hailed and, as it jolted its way along Euston Road to the corner of Gower Street, sat on the edge of the hard leather seat and wondered, not for the first time, why he had come to London and what he was supposed to be doing.

The journey had not been straightforward: his bicycle had developed a puncture halfway to the station; he chained it to the railings of the Catholic Church and ran the rest of the way. He caught the train with five seconds to spare, and it then spent twenty minutes in a siding waiting for the points to clear, while he stared out of the grimy window of his second-class carriage, cursing Born and Wiston. And now his taxi, turning left into the clogged length of Gower Street, rode past the buildings of London University at less than walking speed, as inquisitive passers-by stared through the windows and the meter ticked satirically in its black box. For the fifth time, Thomas tried to work out what Wiston had told him.

If Born had gone off his head and come charging up here in search of details in documents to plant in his spurious visions and sabotage Thomas's research, it should be easy enough to stop him.

But why bother with that? He could simply discount his findings, get another subject for the experiments and start again, apologising to the conference delegates and making sure that next time he would find a guinea-pig with a less highly developed imagination.

But Born was ill, seriously ill, and was either showing the symptoms of a physiological disorder such as epilepsy, or some psychotic condition that was still in its early stages.

The latter would account for the consistency of the visions, and for the differences between the two accounts: Wiston had been right there, at least, which did not stop Thomas calling him, behind his back, a liar, a cheat, a schemer and a necromancer.

Then there was the cassette. Wiston could have made that up, have found a blank and harmless tape, or one with music on it, and be waving it in front of him as a ruinous discovery that would destroy his career, block his promotion, and wreck his reputation as a scientist.

The cassette, if it existed, would show up his pretended scientific principles of observation and experiment as a collection of subjective ploys and self-promoting tactics. If that was what Wiston were trying to prove, it would tie in nicely with what Born had said, or not said, about their strange meetings, dinners and trips to the country together, with all that conspiratorial hedging and hush-hushery.

But if the recording were genuine, what could it tell him? More visions? Horrors he could not put down on paper? Unthinkable, unwritable sights that could only be whispered through the tape-recorder's confessional grille? At the last session Born looked like a man who had had a nasty fright. But what had he seen?

*I must work this out*, thought Thomas as the taxi made its ponderous way down the street, stopping at every amber light. It was an enigma: he had not one single solid fact to put his back against, only suspicions: that Born was neither mad nor evil, but possessed; that Wiston had not set up his deception for any rational reason, but simply as a pure experiment, a trial of strength.

There was one he could be sure of, though: the mirror itself. That must be what he had come to see. Not the books, not the diaries, but the mirror. He should know it well now, after hours of staring at it in the catalogue.

But what did he know about it? What was there to know? Should he think of it as a symbol, an archetype, a model for all that was black and shining? Thomas went through the sequence of events.

Wiston took Born to buy a mirror, and was angry when he had not bought it. Wiston had other mirrors in his rooms, one mirror in particular. They told tales about that mirror, and about Wiston too. Perhaps that was the clue. Born acted strangely in front of anything that showed his face. There was a point in all this, somewhere. If only the taxi didn't take such a devil of a long time! Thomas glanced at his watch. The museum would shut in fifteen minutes. He took money out of his wallet and rapped on the glass partition.

'Can't we get a move on?'

The driver spoke over his shoulder, braking sharply and running up under the tail-lights of a bus.

'Rush hour, guv. Quicker if you walk it.'

They were at the corner of Great Russell Street. The driver let Thomas out, took a five-pound note and drove off without giving him change. Thomas, with the sweat running into his eyes, was pushing his remaining notes back into his wallet when a voice hailed him from further down the street: his anthropologist acquaintance Weiss, with a file of papers under his arm, was coming out of the main gate of the Museum.

'You've come up to see the famous mirror, then?'

Thomas smiled and nodded, and tried to walk past.

'I'm glad I was so persuasive. It's a fascinating object in its own right, let alone its historical associations. But you're too late – the gallery will be shut now, it's after closing-time. Unless you've made an appointment with the curator. But he's got someone with him already, a crazy-looking fellow, I saw them on the stairs –'

Thomas left Weiss by the railings and ran under the plane-trees to the gate, where the guard was blocking the way to incoming visitors, and asking for library cards.

'Cloakroom,' muttered Thomas, as if he had handed in a jewel-box in exchange for a numbered disk, then dashed across the courtyard and up the steps two at a time.

'Library,' he panted to the guard at the top of the steps, glad he had no bags to open and prove their innocence of bombs or crowbars. He searched for Born among the people still in the hall and, not seeing him there, went to the information desk.

'Magic mirrors? Doctor Dee? Aztec artefacts?'

The girl at the counter shook her head.

'We've closed off that part for today. You'll have to come back in the morning.'

'But I have an appointment with the curator.' Thomas found himself using a false foreign accent, and wondering whether to plead a night-flight to Bucharest and an urgent appointment with the Rumanian ambassador.

'Renaissance Gallery. Up the main staircase and follow the signs.'

Thomas nodded, eyes wide open, mouthed 'Renaissance Gallery, most kind, most kind,' edged towards the stairs and stood behind a pillar.

Born's face was white and his hair stood up in spikes as if he had been trying to smooth it with wet hands. He was standing at the foot of the main staircase with the curator, a thin man who was talking volubly with many gestures. Born turned and saw him, but showed no recognition, then followed the curator up the stairs, gripping the banister, not looking to left or right.

Thomas straightened his tie, threw back his shoulders and marched to the foot of the stairs, then stopped and looked back to see which way the arrows were pointing. *Renaissance Gallery* said the sign in orange against buff. He went up boldly, clattering his shoes on the stone steps and pursing his lips to whistle. But his mouth was dry, and no sound came out.

When he got to the top there were mosaic floors all around him, and the sound of approaching tourists being driven out of a nearby gallery, so Thomas stood behind a case of Celtic antiquities and Saxon bronze axe-heads until they had passed the door and gone down the stairs. *I must take another look at those torques some time*, he thought absently, and found himself before a treasure-trove of Roman silver platters, reading the captions. It reminded him of his dinner with Wiston.

Thomas walked on: porcelain in the next room, nothing eye-catching, and then a long blue gallery, silent and empty, with a gleam of silver from the cases on either side. The name *Renaissance Gallery* was over the door. He had come too soon; they were not here: he had overtaken them.

He went slowly now, pretending to observe the silver coffee-pots and cream-jugs, tankards and ladles in their blue velvet cases, and had reached the midway point of the gallery when he was stopped by the sound of singing birds. It came from above his head, from a bright stuffed linnet in a cage of gold wires, with a clock-face below. It was singing the hour.

Thomas stared up at the cage. Then, out of the corner of his eye, he saw a black shape against blue velvet, and as he turned to look at it the velvet gave way to a widening blackness as the back of the case was lifted away. Thomas was on the wrong side of the glass. And there was someone standing at his back who had just entered the room, someone whose head came barely higher than his shoulder.

# *Chapter* 21

'So it was the Georgian relics you wanted to see, was it? Absolutely fascinating little collection, only valuable by association, of course, but once you arrange them together, they shine in each other's light, as you might say, and you end up with something delightfully instructive –'

The curator paused at the first landing, and turned to stare at Born, a mop of grey hair falling over his spectacle-lenses.

'I say, are you feeling all right? You're looking quite off-colour, if you don't mind my saying so . . .'

Born muttered and shook his head, and followed the prattling curator – who later told Wiston that Born seemed to have nothing more wrong with him than an oncoming touch of flu, a feverish headache or a migraine. If he'd known before . . . but some people find the stairs a strain at the best of times, and he had taken them at a trot. They ought to have used the lift. And of course, after closing-time the Museum never felt the same: there were some galleries . . .

'Dr Wiston rang me in the middle of the afternoon. Too late for a proper appointment, but if your deadline's pressing . . .?' The curator turned and gave Born another quizzical look. 'Well, never mind, we're nothing if not accommodating, or try to be.'

Born stumbled on the next flight, and caught hold of the brass rail to steady himself. The curator asked again, 'Do you want to sit down for a minute? No? Quite cheerful?'

Afterwards, to Wiston, he explained how Born had not seemed to know where he was going, and how erratically he moved between the cases.

Born followed him as he threaded his way past the labyrinthine cabinets, with their treacherous surfaces and staring dark circles of bronze. They turned left and right and left again, behind blank screens and through the mouths of open doors.

'Now this is our new layout, and we're proud of it,' said the curator. 'All freshly designed in the latest style: we've taken a leaf or two out of the Americans' book, if the truth were known. And the public response has been good. Oh yes, very good indeed. To set off the silver, we've lined all the cabinets with velvet, white against royal blue. It may look like the Crown Jewels, but where's the harm in that? We've taken some trouble with the lighting, or all you'd ever see would be your face in the glass, and people don't come here just for that. Or do they? Narcissus in the Hall of Mirrors. I wonder.' He tossed his head to flick the hair out of his eyes, and struck a sculptural pose.

They stood at the end of the long dark corridor, lit by the hidden lighting in the cases. Born could see faces marshalling themselves in the silver lids of the tankards, in the sides of the bowls and coffee-pots, in the seals and the medallions. They were in the middle of the gallery, under the hanging birdcage.

'That's one of my favourites. It belongs with the clocks next door, but I brought it in here as a central feature of the display. Enamel and porcelain, eighteenth-century Swiss, but don't you dare call it a cuckoo-clock or I won't let you see what you want.' The curator pinched Born playfully on the upper arm, stepping back when he did not respond. 'That finch is an automaton, built round a bird-fancier's organ. Plays all the tunes of the day, every half an hour. We're five minutes too early, but we'll hear it through the glass.'

He pressed a panel in the wall, and a black doorway opened in front of them.

'Open Sesame!' said the curator. 'I love these little secret passages.' He rattled a bunch of keys that hung from his waist. 'Just like Bluebeard's Castle. I shall open a door one day into a room no one's been in for years, just empty packing-cases full of dust, and suddenly in the corner a face will appear, all covered in cobwebs, and go – ' He thrust his face into Born's, eyes stretched wide open behind the pebble-lenses. 'But I don't want to frighten you. I brought Dr Wiston up here one day – we're old friends of course – and I can tell you . . .'

The first door led to another, in a dark room behind the gallery wall, where pinpoints of light glinted through from the cases.

'I won't bother with the lights, as there'll be plenty from the back of the cases. I must just turn off the alarm system, though. It goes off suddenly and makes you jump out of your skin.' He turned a key in an invisible lock, and a red light came on. He picked up a telephone receiver and pressed a button above the dial. 'Just me in Renaissance, that's right, down in two shakes.' The red light went off. 'Just to keep them happy. All hell let loose, otherwise. Bells, sirens, the lot. Safe as the Bank of

England, they all know that, but you can't be too careful . . .'

He began to undo the catch at the back of the case, feeling with his fingertips and working in the dark. Born stood silently behind him.

Wiston had specified the Georgian memorabilia, kept in the same cabinet as the mirror, for the sake of a little pantomime: Born was to be working on a paper on King George III's insanity, and wished to inspect the artifacts made in commemoration. It was an implausible explanation that the curator had happily accepted.

The back of the case was stubborn, and as he fumbled with it in the darkness, he chattered on.

'Now, the clock I was mentioning, the reason I put it here, you may be interested to know . . .' The curator took out a penknife and levered at the crack. 'When the old king was quite mad, blind and shut up in the palace, they brought him one of these clocks to keep him company. It played the same tunes over and over again, to teach bullfinches to sing. They'd blind them first with a hot needle, quite horrific really . . . but of course, as the king was blind himself . . .'

Born breathed heavily, and leaned against the wall.

'Isn't there a piece of music, quite well-known?' asked the curator, lifting the case-back away. And Born started to sing, he told Wiston afterwards, but he did not think it was the right tune, something older, one he did not know. The back of the case held several shelves, and he concentrated on setting it gently down on the floor.

'Of course, Dr Wiston has quite a collector's interest in the period, I seem to remember. Lots of nice pieces from around the seventeen-eighties, and that fine old mirror in his study. I've always had a liking for that. Talking of mirrors, we have the best of the lot, in this very case: Dee's obsidian mirror, that Walpole said was cannel-coal, the one they called the devil's looking-glass. If you're a good fellow and don't drop anything, I'll give it to you to hold, just for a treat. Strange history. Disappeared for years, then turned up just as poor George III was going mad again. I've often wondered if that wasn't one of Horry Walpole's little plots, as it belonged to him about that time. It's an object of power, no doubt about that. I've always had a fondness for Horry, someone told me once I looked just like him. There!'

The shelves at the back of the cabinet swung half-open on their hinges. Light spilled into the room, and lit the wax tablets, the golden disk with its inscriptions, the sword, the black bowl, the medallion and the mirror in its case.

'Here you are,' said the curator, and gave Born the medallion. 'Turn around and you'll get the light on it.'

Born stood with his back to the corridor, the light falling across his shoulder from the inside of the case. There was a sound of singing birds.

'There goes the clock,' said the curator. 'Just in time. And look, we seem to have an audience.'

Born kept his back to the light.

'I don't know who's on display, us or them,' said the curator. 'They've either got lost or left behind, or . . .' He held out his hand for the medallion.

'Pretty thing, isn't it? Only an historical association that gives it any interest, naturally. Gibbon's sword? No, though it's a nice piece. Burns's wassail bowl? No? Ah, I can see what you want. I believe that's what you were after all the time. Why ever didn't he say so? Old Wiston has his secretive side, I know. Always up to some conspiracy or other.'

He lifted the mirror from its stand.

'Carefully now, I don't want you dropping it. Brittle stuff, obsidian.'

Born kept his back to the light, and bent his head over the mirror.

'I can't think what those people want. They should have left hours ago. They'll be tapping on the glass next . . .'

The mirror was cold, dark and hard. Born held it obliquely, and the light from the corridor fell on to his face. He moved the light within the stone, rocking and tilting it with almost no movement, and the light swung back and forth across his face.

'He started murmuring something,' the curator said to Wiston, 'and I didn't want to interrupt him. I just stood and listened. He's an astonishingly good mimic – if I hadn't been watching him closely, I'd have said it was your voice and you were standing beside me.'

Born began to sway with the movement of the stone: the light grew brighter, and seemed to glow in his face. His back was toward the corridor. The rocking grew stronger.

Then suddenly there was a wordless cry, 'not in his voice or in your voice but coming out of his mouth, and through the glass from the corridor, and he had his face down close to the mirror, and was screaming at something he saw there, and the voice from outside got louder, and he bent his knees and crouched down holding on to the mirror as if something was trying to pull it from him. Then I looked through the cabinet, through the back of the glass, and there was a head staring in, mouth wide open and its face like . . . like the voice. And they were staring at each other in the mirror. I should have turned him round and faced him – what he was staring at was behind his back, and he must have thought . . . it was his own face.'

And then there was another cry, a cry too loud to hear, and Born fell to the floor, knees drawn up into his chest, hands clutching where the mirror had shattered to shards, long fragments of the black stone piercing his body, but no face, no voice, no mirror, only the curator bending over him and Thomas's footsteps running to the door.

# Chapter 22

They took Born to hospital, where a stroke was diagnosed; and some days later, when his condition had stabilized and they had picked out the last splinters of stone, brought him back to a nursing-home close to the college.

During the days that followed, Wiston was pestered and bombarded from all quarters by demands for an explanation of the whole affair, and especially the events of the final moments before Born's collapse.

He called Thomas round for a cup of tea (weak, milkless, China) to get his version of the story. It took him some time to persuade Thomas that he was not himself responsible for the collapse or for the breaking of the mirror. Thomas's version went like this:

'I'd put myself in front of the case in the gallery, the one with the mirror, and waited for the two of them to come. I thought they'd taken a long way round. But then the back of the case started lifting away, and they were just lifting it down when I saw this little character standing next to me, funny little chap he was too, looked

Mexican. They have Indians there, don't they? He was very short, very dark, with straight black hair cut all round like a pudding-basin. Looked like one of those old statues you see, flattish nose, wide cheekbones, long lobes to their ears. I thought he must be one of the gallery guards, come to give me a talking-to for sneaking in after hours. But he wasn't in uniform, and he never said a word. We were both watching too closely.

'Now, the chap behind the glass with Born, the curator fellow, he was talking away nineteen to the dozen and waving his hands about, very demonstrative, pointing to all sorts of bits and pieces, taking them down off the shelves and giving them to Born to hold. I don't know why I didn't try and nip round there and then, or shout or wave to him. I may have tried to move away, but the man beside me was holding me back, keeping me on the spot.

'He wasn't bad, not a bad sort if you know what I mean. There to help, that's what I felt, even if he did pop up like a jack-in-the-box out of nowhere. Not evil, I could tell that. It wasn't his fault, not his fault at all . . .

'Then Born took the mirror. He had his back to us so I couldn't see his face or what he was doing, so I turned round to look at our little friend standing next to me and he had the most astonishing expression on his face I've ever seen. I felt guilty looking at him: you know how in church if you catch sight of someone praying or taking the sacrament, you feel you're breaking in on a mystery. But he had his eyes wide open, like he was concentrating so hard he'd hypnotize you if you looked him straight in the eye. Like someone had asked him a difficult question and he was trying to think of an answer. Not malevolent, nothing nasty about it, more as if he was trying to . . . to put something into Born's head so he wouldn't make a mistake.

'Well, Born turned half round to get a better light on the mirror, just his profile, that's all you could see. And muttering away like someone in church, reading an inscription in the stone. I couldn't hear a word he was saying. Quiet as a church in there, it was, and our friends the curator and the little Mexican fellow like a couple of priests.

'Anyway, up he went to the window, the little fellow, and stuck his nose on the pane, and I went up beside him to see what he was staring at – the whole of this only took a few seconds, though it sounds like half an hour – and I could hear Born whispering away behind the glass. And the funny thing was, you'll think I'm daft, but he sounded just like you. I heard you on the phone as I came in, and I could have dropped dead: it was the same voice. Really uncanny it was.

'So he muttered away and muttered away, with the curator smiling at us through the glass and winking, didn't seem to mind us being there, and just when I thought he was getting near the end, the little Mexican fellow got up on tiptoe, drew a great deep breath and let out the most appalling noise I ever hope to hear – no words at all, just a long scream, the way you'd yell at someone across a valley if you saw a landslide coming, or an avalanche. Well, you wouldn't, maybe.

'And Born started yelling back, like he'd seen it coming too, but couldn't get out of the way in time, and fell sideways like a tree falling, flat down.

'I ran round as fast as I could, to get him up off the floor, but what with all the panels and doors to push past, it took me a few minutes to work out which way to go, and eventually the curator had to come and let me in. Hopping mad about his mirror, he was, said it would cost him his job, and not a word about Born. I found him: he was out cold, frothing at the mouth and spitting blood, worse than the time before. They came up with a stretcher and took him down, but no one saw the little fellow at all.'

Thomas finished his tea, and after a few more remarks went back to his room. Wiston saw him several times in the next few days, and exchanged observations about Born's worsening condition, which Wiston incorporated in his own notes, in these words:

'The telephone call that Thomas overheard was one from my friend and ex-colleague the curator, who had rung me with an explanation, as he saw it, for the breaking of the mirror. Thc fragments, apart from one knife-like piece that had grazed Born's ribcage and cut his hands, were almost all of the smallest size, as if the stone had a gas trapped in it that exploded, or was under some vast internal stress. The only other large fragment was the handle, which remained intact, although the surface was pitted and crazed and had lost its shine. He discounted my idea that the sound of the two voices could have set up a standing wave and shattered the mirror: only the thinnest crystal could be affected like that, and then only by a pure tone to which it could resonate. Nor had it smashed on impact, as Born held it in his hands and it was broken before he hit the ground. He conceded that by twisting it or trying to bend it he might have cracked it in half at an old flaw in the stone, but to reduce it to such tiny fragments would have needed a coal-hammer, as it was the hardest natural glass, quarried from a volcano. But he insisted that it had been shattered by some natural force, acting internally.

"Unless of course you broke it," said the curator.

"Whatever makes you say that?"

"I wouldn't put it past you," he said, and put down the phone.

'Extraordinary remarks of that kind came to me from

all quarters during those days, and were among the reasons that made me decide it would be better if I packed my bags and left the college, at least for the time being.

'Weiss the anthropologist, when I tracked him down, had many things to say: the little man in the museum was evidently an adherent of a Mexican mirror-cult, a latter-day devotee of Tezcatlipoca, who had acted to protect Born from the harm that could come of gazing into the stone. Unfortunately he acted too late, and the mirror and Born's mind were both destroyed. Indeed, he came up with the suggestion that at the instant of the cry, Born's mind and the mirror were in some mystical fashion one and the same: the breaking of the one had broken the other.

"Unless it was your face he saw," said the anthropologist. "That would have shattered them both." This is another example of the gratuitous and uncalled-for rudeness that I have had to ignore. Born's mind was already weakened by the relentless pressure of Thomas' investigations into the Ganzfeld, so why should it not have succumbed quite naturally to the additional shock of seeing an unfamiliar face in the stone? The little man was standing behind him, and though Thomas found him harmless-looking, Born could have associated his face with the one in the vision, and ruptured a vessel in his brain from an astonishment bordering on apoplexy.

'My own thesis, for what it is worth,' Wiston's notes continue, 'is that the figure at the auction, who nearly drove Born off the road and into a ditch, and who out-bid me for the silver mirror (a much older object than the catalogue supposed) was one and the same as the figure in the gallery. That he was malevolent I do not doubt for a moment. And he was not alone. How Thomas could bring himself to destroy his friend's mind so systematically for the sake of a theory, and then refuse to step forward to save him at the last moment, I cannot imagine. Nor can I see how Weiss the anthropologist, clever though he is, can justify the little man's unexplained appearance in the gallery by invoking some American Indian ritualistic hocus-pocus, merely because he has wasted five years of his own life on the same nonsense. There is no evidence that the man was from Mexico at all: more likely an art-thief looking for a loophole in security, commissioned by some transatlantic collector with a lust for obsidian. And how he got out of the gallery at all is a mystery, unless he pulled a peaked cap out of his pocket and walked away in that most impenetrable disguise of all, the uniform of a guard at the British Museum.

'But if he was the man who got in my way before, and if it was his face that appeared to Born in his visions, and his voice that came from the hollow tree, and if, as my friend the curator said, he had been seen standing in front of that very case, day in, day out, for the last few weeks, whenever the gallery was open, what then? I do not know. I do not know.

'Thomas believes they have been the victims of a plot, he and Born, one set up (by me, of course) in the most cynical and unscrupulous fashion to destroy their academic careers, their peace of mind and, in Born's case, his health and sanity. When I ask for evidence he can give me none. I feel I am justified in keeping the cassette to myself, in case an inquest is required and they call me as a witness.

'But I am not afraid of anything they can do: Born's life is over, whether he lives or dies, and so is Thomas's career. The curator will be forgiven and will soon forget the whole affair, and our little friend from the museum has not shown his face again. If he does, I shall tell him to get him behind me.'

## *Wiston's Epilogue*

'These were strange days, between Born's collapse in London and his death, filled with discussions, arguments and silences. People passed me without greeting, with head averted and face cast down. Thomas was the first to stop speaking to me, and others followed him, until I stopped dining in hall and going for my daily stroll around the courts and gardens of the college. Instead I walked to and from the nursing-home where Born was lying, sometimes going in, more often turning at the gate and going back to my rooms, where I had drawn the curtains, shut the shutters and turned the mirrors to the wall.

'The leaves were beginning to drop from the horse-chestnut trees, which are always the first to go yellow and brown and show the autumn coming: there were more and more on the paths each time I went to the nursing-home and back. If one dropped as I passed, I felt tempted to run and catch it before it landed, an old trick to preserve life, to catch a leaf and win a day. But even if the streets were empty, I held back, although I sometimes stood for moments under one tree that had once been badly frosted and was turning early, and waited for the wind to rise and knock a handful of leaves off the top branches. And I would let them fall.

'Born's mother had come up from the country to be near her son, and I passed her often, coming the other way. I saw how rapidly she was ageing: she had stopped tinting her hair – the roots were showing white – as if it would be frivolous to do so while her son was dying. I did not speak to her, but we became friendly in the manner of nodding acquaintances. She knew who I was, but I did not presume on her son's presence to effect an introduction. There were times, at Born's bedside, when I dreaded his coming back to consciousness and giving her to me as a solemn duty, to look after when he died. I could not relish silent visits at which the one subject of conversation would be impossible, and such an errand would not make me wish her any better than I did. She died soon enough, at all events, after passing all his letters on to me. If we met in the nursing-home doorway, I would hold it open for her as she left, and we would smile and nod.

'This evening I met her under the porch, and she did not smile, but held her head down, as if she had been crying and did not want me to see her face. I waited for her to go down the drive and turn the corner into the road, past the tall square brick pillars of the gateposts – there were no gates – and wondered if I should offer to take her home. Then I decided that if I had come all this way on foot I might as well go in and see her son.

'The nursing-home was allied to the college, so I could come and go as I pleased: there were no set visiting-hours, and I did not have to check in and out with the receptionist or ask permission from some officious nursing-sister. Thomas had kept his visits to the mornings, as he was working late at night, so we conveniently missed each other, and did not even pass on the way there or back. It was a comfortable, forbidding building, with a touch of the morgue about its plaster portico and white brickwork. Inside, where there should have been a great sweep of ascending stairs, there was a ramp, floored with linoleum and with low pinewood handrails sweaty to the touch.

'The corridor that led to Born's private room – they did not let one call them wards – was long and smelt of fir-trees, starch and surgical dressings. It was lit along its length with bright fluorescent strips. There were strip-lights, too, in his room, which flickered and blinked like a man with grit in his eye. They had left the blinds open, though it was dark outside.

'I turned off the lights and went towards the bed.

'Born lay motionless on his left side where the nurses had turned him, facing away from the door. They would come to turn him again in an hour, wash him and change his linen. I stood beside the bed and watched him more closely. Now there was so little light on his face, there were no lines or shadows, none of the dark circles under the eyes that had marked the last few weeks.

'His hair fell forward and as I brushed it back from his brow, he opened his eyes. I stood still and waited to see if he would look up or recognize me, but when he did not move again I sat down on the canvas-seated chair beside the bed, my hands folded. I may have begun to sing something, very softly, under my breath. I watched his face. He looked up then, and smiled, a distinct movement at the corners of his mouth. It was hard to attribute any will to this motion, after what the doctors had said about the extent of damage to his brain, but I believe it was willed, whatever they say.

'His hand was lying open, palm up, on the red

blanket, and I laid my finger across it, very gently, hardly touching the skin. His fingers closed on mine, as a baby's might, so at least this reflex was not dead. When I tried to pull my finger away, he gripped harder, so I let it stay where it was. There was little warmth in that grip: the heat in his body had retreated about the heart, which was still beating, though faintly.

'I was glad they had not rigged him up with tubes and wires, pumps and sensors, to keep his life going when his mind had gone. That would have been hard to bear with patience, and I fear I would have unplugged the wires and disconnected the tubes, and let him go by himself.

'The moon was up, and moving across the sky. Soon it would shine through the window on to the bed, and I would see his face. The light was at his feet now, and the mound of bedclothes was a brighter red, but so little red was there in the moonlight that it seemed bleached or washed out. I started to speak, very quietly, under my breath, so that I would not warn the nurses, who did not know that I was there with him.

'I listened to myself as one might listen through the wall to someone murmuring in the next room, trying to catch the voice as it rises and falls. It was not a prayer, what I heard, nor an incantation, more a meditation or a set of instructions. As I spoke, the moonlight followed the line of his body, from the feet to the knees, from the knees to the hips, and up and up the bed until it came to where the mound in the blanket was rising and falling, over his heart.

"You followed me where I took you, and you did not ask where you were going, nor why. Now you are here, you have come to the end of your journey. Your work is done, and you can lie here a while and rest. But you will not rest here long, and when I call you again you must come to me and go wherever I tell you to go, and do what I tell you to do."

'He began to stir under the blanket as if he were too hot, so I loosened his covers and lifted them gently away, and he did not let go of my hand. The moonlight now showed his heart more clearly: its beat seemed stronger and his breathing became deeper and more regular. I went on murmuring under my breath.

' "You were not alone, you were working with others, that I do not know and will not meet. You were working with them and not against them, and you will go on working."

'Now the moonlight was at his throat and I could see the pulses beating on either side as the light came on them. His breathing was stronger, but he had begun to make a little noise in his throat, as if there were still a voice there.

'I looked along his body, whole now and unmarked: the scars of the stone knife had faded, the muscles were sound and responded to the touch. He was paralysed only in the will, struck numb only in the part of the mind that controls conscious, deliberate motion. His eyes were open and looked towards me, but I could not tell if they were focused. I felt a cruel desire to wave my hand in front of them and see if he would blink or turn his head, and worse desires, to pinch him or prod him to see if he would cry out or flinch away. He began to shiver, and I drew the blanket over him.

'Thomas in his kindness and sorrow had brought along his tape-recorder and put it on the table beside the bed, with a little pile of cassettes in bright covers that reflected nothing but his taste in music. From the finger-marks on the cases it looked as if some of his visitors, after stealing the fruit he could not eat, had tried to cover the silent spaces, where conversation should have been, with music he could not hear. There was a cassette in the machine already, but I took it out and replaced it in its case. I had brought my own music with me, and he would hear it.

'He was watching me now, and when I moved my head his eyes followed. I reached into my pocket and took out the cassette he had given me. There was a label on it in his own writing, and I held it up for him to read. That made him flinch, and he would have turned his head away if he could. Instead he closed his eyes, letting the lids fall gently: but I felt that if he could he would have clenched them shut and jammed his fingers in his ears.

'I pushed the button, and a trapdoor opened in the top of the machine. He heard the click, and the deeper sound as I slotted in the little grey oblong with its white paper label. I snapped down the lid and pressed the button to start it playing. His eyelids, still shut, began to quiver: I expected to see tears form and run down his cheeks.

'That would have been quite fitting, as the music, when it started, was the song, "Flow, my Teares", that we had sung together in my room, and that I had recorded to cover his voice. I let him hold my hand again, and it seemed to give him some comfort, I do not know what. The moonlight was full on his face now, and brought out the marks that had vanished in the darkness, or had dropped away when his mind had been absent.

'I listened till the end of the second song, and when the tape had run itself out and clicked to a halt, I sang the last phrase over and, opening his eyes, he sang it back, hardly moving his lips or altering the rhythm of his breathing. When he had finished, he closed his eyes again. I let him rest for a moment, and a face appeared at the square window let into the door, looked in and went away. I sat quite still, and Born did not move. I did not know who it was, and did not want to know: all I can say is that the face came up to the square window from below, as if a little man were lifting himself up on tiptoe to peer through, like a stilt-walker peeping in at an upper room.

'When the face had gone, I started to sing again. It was the song he had sung me in the garden, beside the pool. I sang it slowly, phrase by phrase, and he sang after me in canon, like a round.

'Still singing, and hearing his voice from behind me, I got up off the canvas chair and let go of his hand. I stood at the window and let the moonlight fall on to my face. The moon was very bright and clear, and its face was mild and open, a familiar, friendly face like one I had seen before, and so had Born, but not in the sky.

'I knew now what he had seen in the stone, in the gallery in the British Museum, and over my shoulder in the mirror behind the square piano in my rooms, what he had seen in his madness in every surface that shone and was black, and I knew why it had driven him away and brought him back again.

'I stared at the moon and sang my song. Born sang it with me, a few beats behind, sometimes catching up until we sang in unison, sometimes falling back so that the canon clashed and the chords were untrue. At the end I began again, and he followed me without a pause. The sound went out of the window and came faintly back from the wall at the bottom of the garden.

'There was someone on the lawn, but his face was turned away from us and looking at the moon, and we could not see it.

'Born was beside me now, standing at the window, his blanket fallen on the floor beside the bed, naked in the moonlight. His face was bright, empty and without expression, like the moon itself. His mouth and eyes were open, and he sang.

'At the end of the second verse I turned, still singing, and waited for him to follow me, but he stayed where he was, at the window, singing louder. There was no strength in him or in his voice: he stood, he sang, only with the will I gave him, that no one else would give him. I called to him again when he would not come, but he did not turn. He was watching whoever was there in the garden under the moon, head down, hands resting on the sill, leaning far out.

'I called to him a last time, as the nurse's face was at the door, and the door was opening. But as I went to take him by the shoulder and lead him back to bed there was a cry from the garden, a terrible cry, and he answered it, his hands raised and his voice cracking, and fell forward into the garden, into the light.

'He was dead before he landed, quite dead, I am sure of that, though when I came down into the garden, slowly, along the corridors and down the long ramps, they were holding a mirror up to his face.'

*Also available in Methuen Paperbacks*

---

# Oxford Blood

*Antonia Fraser*

---

A programme on the Golden Kids of Oxford University seems a frivolous prospect, and Jemima Shore, renowned TV investigator, feels she has better things to work on. But a startling confidence from a stranger changes her mind, and draws her to Lord Saffron, at the centre of the closed world of Oxford Society and its peerage. Handsome, disreputable and overprivileged, he is in fact not what he seems: for Jemima has it on excellent authority that he is changeling, and no true heir to the Ives' title and fortune.

As her investigations probe deeper, Jemima becomes involved in Saffron's adopted world of expensive pranks, balls and weekend parties, and finds it thick with sinister intrique and envy. But none of this prepares her for the shock of an attempt made on Saffron's life, and – it seems – her own . . .

'With deft, wry prose and a credible plot, Fraser holds our interest and leaves us clamouring for more Jemima Shore adventures' *Publishers Weekly*

'Dare one say the best Jemima Shore yet . . . Some acid characterisation, much excitement, and lots of fun' *Sunday Telegraph*

# Disorderly Elements

*Bob Cook*

A dazzling thriller of triple-cross at the heart of Western Security.

A Communist Mole in the very top level of British Security! Not even the Philby affair was half so serious. There is near panic in the Cabinet. And the shame of it is that part-time don and veteran M16 agent, Michael Wyman, discovered the shocking truth just as he was about to be sacked, pensionless, from the Firm.

With the threat of the biggest Security scandal yet, Wyman is sent abroad one last time to discover what he can. His only contact is Plato – a highly placed East German who will tell all – at a price. The price is two million pounds and the Prime Minister is devastated. What is going to happen to the policy of drastic cuts in public spending?

'It does for the corridors of British Security what Anthony Jay and Jonathan Lynn did for the Whitehall mob in *Yes Minister*. The humour has the same piquant irreverence.' *The Oxford Times*

'Spy-fi has unearthed a splendid new recruit in Mr Cook' *The Observer*